MW01094586

James P. White

I Am Everyone I Meet
Random Encounters on the Streets of Los Angeles

Tabloid Books Inc.

TABLOID BOOKS, INC.
PMB 272, 1223 WILSHIRE BLVD.
SANTA MONICA, CALIFORNIA 90403
www.tabloidbooks.com
ISBN# 1448640148

Cover Image: *The Writer*, Photo-collage, Jules White

for Don Bachardy

Introduction

Before I came to Los Angeles I decided to write a book called "The Spiritual History of Los Angeles." It was to be a detailed survey of spiritual developments in Los Angeles from the time of the Indians to the present and was to include brief comments about all the spiritual books written by Angelenos. I began work on it as soon as I arrived, going to various libraries, reading about the Indians so mistreated by the early Christians, and taking notes on books by several L.A. theologians. It did not take me long to realize how many years it would take to complete such a work and how easily it could fail under its own weight. There is just too much material, no matter how interesting it is.

Instead I began to write about the strangers I met daily in Los Angeles, from all walks of life. Of course, I was one of those strangers myself. At first I decided to write only about emotions I saw people expressing; I did not talk with them. I would walk up and down busy or isolated streets, looking closely at everyone. Then I began to approach and talk with people and soon realized that personal interaction was integral to what I was trying to do. Living in Santa Monica I had many conversations with the homeless in Palisades Park and on the Promenade, then I widened my focus. Soon I began to *purposefully* write about strangers I met throughout the city. I would head out to meet them, traveling to Beverly Hills, downtown L.A., east L.A., Hollywood, the Valley—as many places as I could. I was not sure why I was writing such material, but it interested me.

After a while, though, I understood why. How many strangers have I passed in my life, not once but many times, and known nothing about their lives? How many times when I was passing these people, were my thoughts absorbed with myself? I ignored people I did not know. This book is about approaching part of my life by meeting and listening to strangers tell about their lives. It is about their lives touching mine, and mine touching theirs, so that their stories become something important for me to learn about.

The dialog in this book is all true.

This larger whole extends past any city of course. But it is in the city that conditions exist that jostle people up against each other so that they actually touch—in traffic, on busy sidewalks, in restaurants, gyms, coffee shops, parks, churches, etc. This place where people touch is where they feel, not only the impact of the lives of others, but of their own.

The writer Christopher Isherwood told me about this once, at the end of his life. We were sitting on the terrace of his house in Santa Monica which overlooks the Pacific Ocean. We spoke of people in his life—his mother, brother, famous writers and actors, and others. Suddenly he was moved by something he thought. He could not hold back his emotions. "Oh Jim!" he said, "The people that I've known—they've touched me. They've *touched* me." He said this because he felt it so strongly at that moment and he also said it so that I would know. Our lives touch each other. Being aware of this touching is what living is all about.

It is the subject of this book.

Last night, riding in a taxi from the airport to my apartment, I began a conversation with the driver. He had lived in Moscow during the Communist period. He told me how beautiful Moscow was, of the simplicity and pleasure of not having to buy an apartment (and Moscow is all apartments he said), of having health and dental care paid for. He looked back on the Communist period as delightful, then spoke of the super rich building multi-million dollar homes outside the city now. He spoke of the financial inequality that made him leave Russia. I had never heard anyone praise the communist system and was not sure what I thought of what he said. But his nostalgia was real and the way he looked back on his experience touched me. He couldn't afford to buy an apartment or a house in L.A., so he thought of the Russia that he left.

What is the Los Angeles that emerges from talking with these people? I see it more clearly using their eyes as well as my own. First, it is a place to pursue the American Dream. Those I talked with dismiss other U.S. cities. Los Angeles, to them, is recognizable, accessible, and famous—some place they can live that does not seem so foreign. A German carpenter comes because he has heard of mansions being built in Malibu. A Venezuelan seeks political freedom. He is afraid to even visit the South. A Mexican joins millions of his kind. A Brazilian valet car parker tells of living with seven roommates in a one-bedroom apartment in Palms while each pursues making money. Two Australians speak of pursuing film careers. And all of us are shoulder to shoulder.

The joy of the experience comes from the recognition that we are not entirely alone and shut up in our individual worlds. Most of the time we take what is happening around us as background for our thinking. Everyone we pass, however, is immersed in thoughts just as we are. Dealing with strangers in any situation brings forth an unknown aspect of our daily lives that offers something new, powerful, and affective to each of us.

Seeing the world as filled with strangers who threaten us or seeing it as filled with other people who are like us and who interest us, makes a difference.

It isn't necessary to read the sections in any particular order. They are arranged as spontaneously as I met the strangers. Regardless, these people have touched my life in some way, at one moment, as I have theirs.

§

I need to take a bus to pick up my car which is being repaired. I walk three blocks from my apartment to the promenade and down to the bus stop at Santa Monica Boulevard.

I don't see a bus coming. A short, stocky Chicano sits on the arms of the only bench where one waits for a #304 bus. His feet rest on the seat, taking up space where someone could sit. It would be awkward for anyone to sit on the bench beside him. Several people who possibly would like to sit down are standing around. I sit, anyway, his shoes inches from my thigh. I stare directly at him, to make him feel uncomfortable. Doesn't he realize he's taking up the entire bench because of the way he's sitting? Someone else beside him might want to sit down.

He avoids looking at me.

"Hello," I say, deciding to confront him just as he does me.

He barely nods.

"Where are you going?"

"Home."

"Where is it?"

"East L.A."

"Your English is good," I say.

He shakes his head. "No," he says, "Not good."

"Yes, it is. Can you understand me?"

"Yes."

"It's good. Where do you work?"

"At a restaurant in Pacific Palisades."

He has to repeat "Pacific Palisades" several times for

me to understand his pronunciation. "What's the name?" I ask.

"The Bistro."

"Yes, I've been there."

He smiles broadly. "You've eaten there? When?"

"A month ago."

"I was there," he says, "busing tables."

"Why are you waiting here if you work in the Palisades and live in East L.A.?" I ask.

"I take off because I lose bus pass. I go by the Big Blue bus office."

"Oh," I say. "So it's located here."

"Before I worked at the Bistro," he says, "when I come to L.A., I work at Japanese restaurant. They make me learn Japanese."

"You learned Japanese?"

"Yes, I not know English."

"Yet you speak Japanese?"

"Yes."

"My goodness," I say. "You know Spanish, English, and Japanese. Say something in Japanese."

He says several phrases. "I talk to cooks," he says, "and the owner. They Japanese."

He laughs. I laugh, too. It is funny to both of us.

"When was that?" I ask.

"Five years ago."

"Was it hard to learn?"

"Yes," he says, "very hard."

The bus arrives and we stand up and walk over to it. I stand back for him to get on before me because he was at the bus stop when I got there. Suddenly it is crowded.

"No, no," he says, "you first."

"No, you first."

"No—you, please," he says, very politely.

I get on, pay, and sit on the bus. As he walks along the aisle past me, he stops. His eyes light up. He hesitates, then touches me on the shoulder and smiles. I smile back. For one moment, we make contact just because of the slightest things we know about each other. Imagine his learning Japanese— and imagine the improbability of his telling me about it.

§

While sitting at the Big Blue Bus stop in Santa Monica between 3rd and 4th Streets, every minute makes me impatient. The carefully designed metal benches don't much matter. The bus stop itself means, come sit here. Do nothing. Don't look directly at anyone. *Wait.*

I look hopefully toward Ocean Avenue where the next bus will turn onto Santa Monica Boulevard. It would interest me to know where the other three people who are waiting, are going—to which apartment or what job or store. I'm curious about the bags they carry and everything I don't know about their lives. I glance at each of them.

They don't like my looking.

The busy sidewalk makes me aware that everyone else is moving and I'm sitting still. Finally a bus rolls around the corner, and not a moment too soon. I queue up where I think the bus will stop, but of course it edges a few feet farther. I try to get on as soon as I can, pay, and take a side seat facing the sidewalk. Passengers begin to choose empty seats around me.

As they do, I notice that two men walking down the aisle are the spitting image of each other. One is obviously the father and thirty years older. Both wear kipas. As the son sits by the large window, he sinks into his seat. His body literally scoots down, making his dark coat collar rise up around his neck. His legs, too, withdraw up into his pants. The father sits with his back erect and stares straight ahead.

Suddenly the son reaches across and takes the father's hand. The father lets him. Leaning over as he would do if he were proposing, the son puts his other hand on top of the hand that is holding his father's. He begins to stroke his father's hand affectionately-- no, with lovingness. His entire face clouds with emotion. His eyes soften, his cheeks color, his mouth pooches. He seems oblivious of the other people on the bus. He rubs the hand as the bus lurches to a start.

The father sits stiffly.

Perhaps the father has received bad news about his health, I think. Is the son showing concern about that? Maybe. Or has the son done something that needs to be forgiven and rubs the hand to soften up the father? It is impossible to tell. But it is the act that matters, this prolonged touching of the hands of these two men.

As we ride along the blocks, the son caresses his father's hand. The physical action holds powerful psychological feelings. Especially because I did not know my father.

Not a word is exchanged. Neither looks at the other.

My heart is touched whether my sympathy goes to the father for his bad news or to the son for having done something that the father disapproves of. My heart goes out to their intimacy.

§

I am stopped at a light on Broadway in downtown LA.
I glance to my right, at a young man about 17 or 18, standing
outside a women's dress shop. He is a tall, slender Chicano,
wears old jeans, a baggy white tee shirt and basketball shoes.
His glistening black hair is spiked. I notice his eyes. With
one hand he grasps the handle of a buggy which holds a child
under the age of one. But he does not look at the baby. Nor at
the shoppers walking past. He stares far, far away, not at the
traffic or the stores or me. What he sees is not in front of him.
It is as if he is looking into thin air. A frown on his lips seems
filled with regret. He wants to be somewhere else. He wants
to be doing something else. His expression says he does not
want to be standing there with the child and buggy. The light
changes. I drive on.

§

My son Jules, who is 26, is paying for two shirts at a
trendy shop in Westwood. I stand beside him at the counter,
waiting. The sales lady, about twenty, is folding the size extra
large tee shirts. Jules pulled them off in the dressing room,
carelessly not turning them right side. She begins to fold one
of them, wrong side out, getting ready to put it into a plastic
bag. I watch to see if she will correct what she is doing. She
pays no mind. I reach over and take the other shirt. I turn it
right side out to show her, then fold it. She glances at me. I
have corrected what she just did. She frowns. "It's much nicer
this way when you put it on later," I say. I think she should

know this when she waits on other customers. She reaches over, takes his credit card without answering, and rings up the sale. Her hands move quickly. She finishes the sale without speaking. She does not appreciate having been corrected. Nor does she care if he is a return customer or not as she hands him the bag with the clothes and receipt and turns her back to us.

§

I get on a bus, coming from picking up a new pair of reading glasses. Shortly after I sit down in the middle seat at the rear of the bus, I silently watch the stores pass and see the profiles of the people in their seats. They are in different postures, some bent over, some very erect, some arms on the tops of the seats, some resting on laps. Suddenly I realize how beautiful the postures of these people are, their arrangement, their silhouettes and the gentle movements they are making. The view is exquisite, like a gorgeous painting, only it contains perfection. I sit still, watching, until my feeling passes, which takes half a minute.

§

My car is ready at the auto upholstery company in suburban Los Angeles. The night before last someone cut into the plastic back window of my convertible and I am having the window replaced. The first price quoted was $810, then finally it was lowered to $450. The fabric top with the plastic window looks fine again.

I go inside the building to pay for the repair work. It is

5 p.m., quitting time. A stocky Chicano stands by the worn out desk. He grins, but with a gesture makes it clear he does not speak English. "Is the manager here?" I ask.

He nods. "No Englishe," he says and hurries out. A moment later the manager walks in ahead of him.

"Your car is ready," the manager who also is Chicano, says.

"Good." I pull a check out of my billfold.

"Do you have cash? I prefer cash," he says.

"No."

"All right."

I take my pen and fill in the amount on the check that is on the bill he hands me. The $450.00 includes tax I guess.

"Make it out to him," he says, pointing to the other Chicano.

"What?" I ask, "to him?"

"Him. Alfredo Gonzales."

"Alfredo Gonzales?"

"Yes."

I wonder why he doesn't want me to write the check to the company. And who is Alfredo Gonzales? "OK," I say. I don't ask more. Alfredo looks over as his name is mentioned. He watches me.

I fill in the name and hand the check to the manager. "Thanks," I say. I think, this is not how we do business in the U.S.

"Thank you," he says and puts the check into his billfold, not in the register. Then he smiles broadly at me.

I think, as I leave, maybe it is how we do business now, since I just did. Sometimes it's hard deciding whether to be polite or honest.

§

Leaving my table at a restaurant in Venice, I walk to the narrow hallway with two restrooms. I try the door to the men's, but it is locked. The women's is four feet down the hall.

A chubby young blond man wearing a plaid sports coat is red cheeked as he enters the hallway and stops, seeing me ahead of him. He is in a hurry. "Is someone in the men's?" he asks.

"Yes."

"The women's is the only one with a lock that works," he says.

I start to tell him that if you push your finger into the men's lock, it functions fine. It's just that the covering over the button is missing. He looks away, not interested.

The door opens. A buxom blonde leaves the women's.

"Go ahead," he says, motioning impatiently.

Part of me hesitates, disliking his telling me to do something I ordinarily wouldn't. But I know that he will use the women's if I won't. I do what he says. I open the door, shut it and press in the lock. The pile of wadded paper towels on the floor surprises me, as does the general disarray of the room. Water has splashed onto the tile floor and soggy Kleenex are wadded in the sink. I had always thought women's restrooms would be cleaner than the men's.

A minute later, I turn around and leave the bathroom. I am slightly embarrassed because I see an older woman standing on the other side of him, waiting. She is surprised that a man is leaving the women's restroom.

The chubby guy's blue eyes light up, seeing me, and he pushes past, going into the women's before her. He shuts the door. I continue, noticing her eyes and posture as I pass.

§

I am walking along Doheny in Beverly Hills when a horn blares. Someone is pressing on it again and again and again, disturbing everyone. I turn to see what's going on. A woman with scraggly grey hair and using a walker is making her way across the traffic. She is only midway through the first lane and the light already has changed to green. She should not be crossing the street using a walker. She is holding up everyone and has a lane and a half to go. It will take her another light at least to get to the other side. Maybe two. Cars in both lanes will have to wait. Traffic will pile up.

The horn blares, upsetting her, slowing her down. I can see how shaky she is.

I realize all the fuss comes from one car--a shiny black Cadillac. Then I see the driver. An elderly woman about the same age as the one who is crossing sits behind the wheel. She scowls as she presses the horn over and over while the old woman using the walker tries to hurry. The woman in the Cadillac is not going to let her get away with it.

§

Richard, the friendly young actor behind the register at the gym, takes my ten dollar bill to pay for a new lock and counts out change. Just as he finishes, a middle age businessman wearing a suit and in excellent shape hurries up to the counter. "I'm going to work out now," he says, "but there's a chance I could have a stroke. My doctor says I should tell you."

Robert does a double take. I do, too.

"See how drained my face is? I need to get my blood pumping."

The guy's face does have a purplish tint.

"Your doctor says you might have a stroke?" Robert asks.

"I feel like shit," the man says.

"I don't know about working out then," Robert says.

"I have to. Look at my complexion. See how drained it is?"

"If your doctor says you are about to have a stroke, you can't work out." Robert speaks firmly, suddenly standing up straight.

"You can't keep me from it," the man says. His entire demeanor changes.

Robert's eyes narrow. "Yes, I can," he says.

"I paid my membership. You can't stop me."

"If it's bad for your health, I can." He hesitates, his voice very tense. "And I will."

"The doctor says it's good for me to work out, but I *could* have a stroke."

Robert isn't persuaded.

"I *have* to work out."

Robert stands quietly mulling over the situation.

"He's OK," I say, "let him work out. He knows what his body needs."

Neither of them speaks. They suddenly are confronting each other about whether or not Robert has the power to stop him. The guy's stroke has become secondary.

"It's OK, Robert," I say. Something about the guy tells me that he needs attention. That's why he came up and told us his situation. He wants sympathy.

Robert nods and waves the man past. Then he looks at me and shakes his head.

§

I am on the back of a bus, coming from Hollywood. Beside me rides a couple in their early thirties. The man's blond mustache and sideburns are trimmed. I see his profile. He has his left arm around a Chicano woman whose eyes are closed. He massages her shoulder slowly. He begins to chew on a fingernail of his right hand. I can see how close down he has chewed the nail already. On the next seat are a bedroll and a thirty year old suitcase that must be theirs.

He pats her shoulder. Then he begins to chew on another fingernail. His eyes as he scrapes his nail with his teeth look tense.

Occasionally, our eyes meet.

I take forty dollars from my billfold and put it in my shirt pocket. I will give it to him as they get off the bus. I understand the responsibility he feels for both of them. I think I am giving the money because he cares for her. If he were alone, I'd probably give him nothing.

He rides several blocks, chewing on his nails, then rubbing on her shoulder and arms. Once she looks up at him. He brushes back the hair on her forehead.

"Where are you from?" I ask the next time he glances at me.

"Montana. I've been in L.A. a year and a half. But I

lost my job at a restaurant in the valley."

I notice faded tattoo's on his arms. He has deep set blue eyes and he looks like he's worked hard all of his life.

"How long did you work there?"

"Six months. The manager was not very nice. It was in Sherman Oaks."

"Why wasn't he nice?"

"He lied to people."

"How did you get there every day?"

"On the bus. I've looked for another job, but haven't found one. We just got kicked out of our apartment in Hollywood. It was $515.00 a month. I don't have it this month."

"Where are you going?"

"To the beach. We'll live outside a while. I've done it before."

"When did you do it?"

"When I was thirteen."

"Thirteen? How did you survive?"

"I just did. We're OK. I have to be extra careful because of her."

"You're free," I say.

"Not really. But we have each other. And look here." He brings out a sheet of paper. "Here's the schedule for the free meals in Santa Monica."

"Yes," I say, "I see." I read it and hand him back the sheet.

"You can keep it," he says. "I can get another."

I realize that he thinks I am homeless, too. "OK," I say.

He nods, then begins to rub her shoulder. She opens

her eyes and looks at him.

"Thirteen was awful young," I say.

"Yes. I learned a lot. But I got kicked out at home when my mom died. I didn't have a choice. Here's our stop." He reaches over and picks up the bedroll, then the suitcase. She gets up. "I'll see you," he says.

I nod. "Hey," I say, "here." I take the folded money from my pocket and hand it to him. He is surprised, but glad.

I watch them get off the bus. They stand at the curb outside the window and she looks at the folded money he holds. He is about to unfold it and see how much it is, then he glances up and sees me looking at them. He is embarrassed. He blushes. He puts the bills in his back pocket. He waves bye.

The bus pulls out. I stand up, ready to get off at the next stop. I wonder where they will sleep.

§

A young heavy set man walks ahead of me on the street. Instinctively I know he is headed toward a nearby park. He eats something I can't identify from a Styrofoam container. Fries maybe. A homeless man passes by, going in the opposite direction. "I've got the munchies," the chunky guys says. "See you later." Half a block farther he pauses, sets the container on top of a trash can and says, "Stay!" to the Styrofoam. It blows onto the sidewalk as he walks on. I feel irritated that he has littered, but realize his "Stay!" means he feels guilt about not disposing of it as he should. He walks ahead; I follow. Perhaps it is more curious that I am following him, than what he is doing. We cross a street and reach a park. There, he suddenly hurries over to a trash container and takes the peeling from

17

half a grapefruit—something that should have been put inside as well, yet was set on top. He twirls it in his hand as he walks along. What is he going to do with that? I wonder. Then he brings it to his lips and takes a bite, his first, as he saunters, enjoying himself.

§

A man stands at the street corner of Arizona and Second. He is smiling, really smiling, his lips spread widely, his teeth bared. His eyes make contact with everyone who passes, including me. I glance at him. His eyes lock on mine, his lips frozen in the smile. He turns his head, continuing to stare as I pass. His eyes have nothing to do with his lips. It is the most sinister thing I've seen all day. No one in his right mind would smile for more than a minute. He knows it. And eyes and lips smile together.

§

As I get on the bus, I step back because the driver is honking and the blare hurts my ears. It is as loud as music at a rock concert. Like the siren of an ambulance. He does not stop. He presses on the horn, warning a car in front. The car doesn't really seem in the way. I enter, pay and go to the back to get away from the sound. As he pulls out, he honks again, three times. I lean toward the aisle and look at the driver. He is angry about something. The noise makes everyone on the bus nervous. At the next stop, he honks as he pulls into it, then honks as he pulls out. He presses on the horn for a long while.

I look out the front window, but see nothing in his way. He honks again, and again, and again. I glance at the man beside me. He smiles, then shrugs his shoulders. I stand up to get off the bus at the next stop.

§

It's impossible to go out in Los Angeles all day and not be confronted with the homeless. I've been watching a middle aged black guy riding across from me on the bus to Santa Monica. He's been meticulously counting his change, which is six pennies. He cleaned each coin with the dirty page of a section of book he is carrying, then stuck them into his pants pocket. He also has taken out three one-dollar bills, unfolded them, and now looks down at them. I can smell him—an unclean stench.

But something tells me he is gentle. I reach over and slowly take the three dollars from his hand.

He is startled, turns around, and looks at me. I am grinning and hand them back to him.

He laughs. We both think it is funny—my stealing from him. He keeps a smile, as I do. He refolds the bills and slides them into his pocket.

I suspect that if I really wanted them, he'd give them to me. He has that in his eyes.

He begins to eat Cheetos, holds up the bag up high and lets the Cheetos drop into his mouth. Then he wads up the empty package and sticks it into a plastic sack beside him.

The veins in his arms are prominent and he has a beard and mustache. No body fat without going to the gym. Much of his head and face is covered with black wiry hair. He has a patrician nose and deer-like eyes. He's remarkable looking. He pulls a bar of white soap from his pocket, looks at me, and smiles.

I can't resist. "Tell me what's in your sack," I say.

He pulls out a shirt, a pair of wool gloves, and an old tie. All are dirty. I notice that he leaves one item in the bag. "What's that?" I ask.

"A crack pipe," he says. He raises it half way out so I can see.

"Oh? I've never seen one."

"Never? I'm an addict."

I look at his arms. He sees me and holds them out, pointing to knots along the veins where he has shot up and scarred.

"My father and mother were, too. I became an addict at fifteen." His voice is low and soft.

"Where do you live?"

"South central LA. But I've been homeless since I was eighteen."

"Why?"

"I have depression."

"Psychological problems," I say.

"Yes. Mental." He nods, reassured that I know what he means.

His feet are wrapped up in some kind of thick cloth rather than in socks. "What is that?" I ask, pointing.

"I don't like socks. I cut up my shirts and use them for socks. The shoes fit better."

I see that the running shoes are too big for him. "What are the pages of the book?" I ask.

"I got it in high school," he says. "I haven't finished

it."

"You've carried it all these years?"

"Yes. I'm going to finish reading it."

He likes answering the questions. "How old are you?"
I ask.

"Thirty-three."

"The age of Jesus when he died," I say.

"I think he was 32. I'm going into rehab again. I've
been thinking about it."

"Where are you going now?"

"To Venice Beach. Day before yesterday I met this
man. He asked me what I would do with him. I told him
'anything'. I went to his house. Out by Knotts Berry Farm.
I woke up the next morning in the park in Santa Monica.
He gave me two pills the night before. I blacked out. I don't
remember anything that happened. I lost my jacket."

"What did you two do?"

"I don't know. I'd go back and get my jacket, but we
could fight. I don't want the police. I don't want to go to jail."

"Are you gay?" I ask.

"I don't tell anyone about me and love. Not even my
mama. I keep it in here." He points to his heart. "I keep all that
stuff in here like in a bottle of champagne." He leans closer.
"Can I get a dollar from you?"

"Later," I say.

"I panhandle," he says. "I can make money anywhere.
You could panhandle."

"I'd like to try," I say. "Have you ever walked from
Santa Monica to downtown LA? I'd like to do that."

"I've walked a lot farther than that. To the valley. You
could walk downtown, but not to the valley. It's dangerous."

"You walk a lot," I say.

"I walk everywhere."

"You're free."

"I feel free like in the song, 'Home of the Free and the Brave'."

"You are free," I say. "I have to get off at the next stop." I take out my wallet, fold a bill so that he can't see and hand it to him. "Don't look at it," I say. I don't want his thanks. I feel good giving him the money.

He puts it into his pocket. I get off and he does, too. He follows along with me. "You know where you are?" he asks. The traffic is whizzing past in the street.

"Yes," I say. "The Promenade. It's nice here."

"Yes."

He slows, then stops walking. "Well, I'm going the other way. You want to go with me?"

"I can't," I say.

I put out my hand. He shakes it.

"Thanks," he says, smiling.

"Thank you," I say.

He hesitates then seeing that I'm willing, he spreads his arms and gives me a tight hug. The smell does not bother me. "I love you," he whispers, bringing his face close enough to kiss me. "I really love you."

"I love you, too," I say. He lets go, then smiles and walks away in the opposite direction.

I feel that I do love him. Who else, I think, would have told me he loves me in the space of half an hour? And who, when I got on the bus, would have believed it was going to happen? I ask myself what I can learn from him.

My college roommate, an only child, would throw the

change from his pockets into the waste basket when he came
into the room. Every three months he discarded all his clothes
and bought new ones. One weekend he bought a Mercedes,
decided he didn't like it, and traded it off in a few days. After
he graduated, he went to divinity school, but was not ordained.
He never worked. He moved in with his mother, worried about
his health, and when she died, he said he was going to spend
all of his money. Four years later, penniless and ill with AIDS,
he plunged off the balcony of his penthouse, to his death.

     His point zero was not nearly so low as this homeless
man's.

§

     An overweight man walks just ahead of me on
Wilshire, close to the L.A. County Museum. The waist size of
his blue jeans must be sixty or seventy inches. When I was a
boy he could have been in a freak show at the state fair. His
shirt looks pressed and immaculate. His arm is wrapped around
the shoulder of a thin blonde woman. They look about thirty.
Shorter than he is, she hooks one of her fingers into a belt loop
of his jeans. Just below it, his butt cheeks are mammoth.

     She wears gold rimmed glasses and has a pale
complexion with a rosy hue. She smiles directly into his eyes.
Then she pats him on the shoulder and moves her face in closer
to his. He likes her, too. His care shows in the lightness of his
step. They seem buoyed along with their emotions, floating,
like balloons. Her mouth registers the changes in her heart.
Her face has gaiety. She is very pretty. Her character shines
through. As they walk, encircling each other, the strong wave
of happiness they create, spreads to me as well.

§

Four young men wearing laundered white shirts, colorful silk ties and dress slacks come boisterously into the locker room at the gym, choose lockers and begin to undress. I pay little attention to what they are saying because it is loud. I have seen the biggest one of them working out hard, keeping in perfect shape in his late twenties. He appears to be their natural leader. A tall, buff guy with a buzz cut, asks him a question I don't hear. "Yeah," the big guy answers, "he's OK now."

"What did he say to you?"

The answer is something I don't hear, either, although I am listening.

"He said that! No wonder you got upset."

"You didn't tell me he did that to you," another adds . "You said…"

All of them stop undressing and huddle around Mr. Perfect. They have heard something they won't leave alone. The big guy has been put down by the boss. It's as if they have found a weakness of his to attack. They circle like sharks going after a drop of blood.

"What'd you say back?" one asks.

"Well," he says, "in context it wasn't so bad. He acted like he was joking."

"It doesn't sound like a joke."

"He was with Richard for an hour yesterday," another says.

"And he had lunch with Dr.Perkins at Spago."

"At eight o'clock this morning he said he was going to pick the project manager for K systems tomorrow. Shelly told me that."

"I saw him in his office as we left," one says. "He was on the phone."

"He was there at nine last night. He had dinner sent in from Bruno's."

"I met with him five minutes this morning. He was on the phone with Tyler when I came in."

"Have you seen the new wheels?"

"Of course."

I am finished dressing. As I leave, they are still adding information about the boss.

§

I am at lunch with an actress who once was widely recognized for her talent. She is describing filming on a current project in Jersey. "These older actors are in a fix," she says. "In order to look like themselves, they can't grow old naturally, so they have a lot of surgery done. A whole lot. On film they look pretty good and are kind of recognizable. But up close they look like freaks. Their faces become exaggerations of what they were: huge, huge lips, big eyes, emaciated... It's hard not to burst out laughing."

§

I am visiting a friend in Pasadena. On the bulletin board above the mail boxes in his apartment house someone has anonymously posted a note. *You have hurt us tenants. You have increased our base rates 287%. You have made our lives uncomfortable with water and electrical problems. You are a*

25

rat. We trap rats.

I think about taking down the note and throwing it into the trash. I do not believe in anonymous notes and don't agree with the sentiments. I leave it, for the landlord to deal with as he has to.

He probably knows who wrote it.

§

I pay fifty-five dollars for an hour and a half Thai massage. I lie in my boxer shorts on a thin mat that is covered with a blue cotton sheet. The Asian masseuse, dressed in a baggy white Nike workout suit, wears oversize dark sunglasses. She is barefoot. Her toenails are painted blood red. She motions that she does not speak English. She asks, "Massage hard? Medium? Soft?"

"Medium," I say.

She points to my stomach and I lie flat on it. She climbs on top of my thighs, kneading my back and neck with her fingers. I am very aware that while sitting on me she touches me with parts of her body that anyone would consider private. Like she is riding a horse. She presses down against me and rubs. Finally she climbs off me, sits by my side, and has me turn on my left. She squeezes my arm. "You hot?" she asks.

She is not attractive to me. I came in for a massage. "I'm fine," I say.

She goes back to work. Then she sits up, unscrews the lid and drinks from a large plastic bottle of water. She sets it down and replaces the top. She massages five minutes, unenthusiastically. "You hot?" she asks.

"I'm fine," I say. I sit up.

"No hot?"

"No sex," I say.

"No, no. This,"—and she blows air through her lips like a fan. "You hot?"

"Sure," I say because she wants me to.

"You hot?"

"Yes."

"One minute. I fix." She gets up and leaves the room. When she returns she finishes her bottle of water.

The air conditioning kicks in and the room begins to cool. Perhaps she is hot, I think. Maybe I was wrong. I concentrate as she takes a wet cloth and wipes my back. Then she raises my arm. I realize that she knows what she is doing. Her fingers and knuckles press at places that suddenly feel sore along my side.

She positions me on my back and begins to massage my right leg. She leans her torso against the bottom of one of my feet, my leg bent at the knee and with one of her feet pressed against my inner thigh. She presses all along the muscles. "You like?" she asks.

"Uh huh."

"Feel good?"

"Yes."

"Tell me it feel good."

"Feels good," I say.

"Yes, yes. Feel good."

This time she crosses one of my legs and with her body, finds another way to stretch my ham string as far as she can. "Yes, that's good," I say to encourage her. I wouldn't be surprised if I couldn't walk the next day.

"Yes, good."

"Yes."

She sits up. The room has gotten much cooler. "One minute." She leaves and comes back carrying a can of Coke. She sips from it. "I hot," she says. "I tired." She sits on the floor beside me.

I wonder if she can go on.

"How many massages have you done today?"

She holds up her fingers. *Seven.*

"How could you do seven? Mine is an hour and a half long."

"I come eight in morning until eleven at night."

"Eleven? That's fifteen hours."

"Yes. I ride bus home—two hours. I sleep, get up at four. I eat, wait for bus, ride back. Two hours. Here eight morning."

"That's terrible."

"I so tired," she says. "I hot. Sick. Feel."

I touch her arm. Her skin is feverish.   "Are you sick?" I ask.

"Yes. Very sick. No food. I go home late last week. Stores closed. I no food. I hungry."

"How long do you sleep?"

"Three hours. Not enough. All massages today medium. I glad, but I need sleep. I upset."

"You must be."

How can I help her? I wonder. She would be in trouble if I stopped the massage. But I don't want to make her more tired or catch anything she might have. Stopping would anger the eagle-eyed boss I saw as I entered. The masseuse obviously had to have me complain that the room was too hot; her being uncomfortable wouldn't matter.

"You work?" she asks.

"Yes."

"How long?"

"Seven hours," I say.

"You lucky."

Her jet black hair is very thin. She has balding spots the dye can't hide. She is much older than she appears at first. She must be sixty. Her mascara is exaggerated.

"Are you married?" I ask.

"No husband."

"Children?"

"No."

I imagine her giving massages all day, waiting for the bus, going to her apartment. Sleeping alone. Not more than three or four hours, getting up, dressing, riding the bus to work.

The things I do not know about her would be even more telling than those I do. Surely they would explain how she could lead such a life. Not speaking English has to be part of the reason.

Regardless, her misfortune makes me feel fortunate, even if that is selfish, and surely it is. Hearing her problems and caring does not mean I should try to solve them. Imagine if she tried to solve mine.

I smile as she continues at a slow pace. "You come back," she says. "I like. You feel good. You regular customer now. Yes?"

"Yes," I answer, unenthusiastically.

"You regular customer," she repeats. "I like you."

§

I walk into the dressing room at the gym, feeling like talking. A young guy not far from the locker I usually pick is changing into his gym clothes. His tomato red sports shorts are dingy and clash with a baggy green tee shirt that swallows him. His spiked blonde hair is peroxided and sticks up too far by several inches. I wonder if he would trim it if he could really see it. He's not in very good physical shape.

"Someone left a dirty Q tip," I say, pointing to one on top of the orange bench. I think that if it were a towel, I'd put it in the bin, but I leave the Q tip.

"Hmm," he says, his voice friendly. "Are you from here?"

"I rent an apartment," I say.

He nods.

"What do you do?" I ask, thinking that I have no hint from his looks.

"I work in Hollywood."

"Are you a writer?"

"Yes."

"What do you write? Screenplays?"

"Yes," he says, lowly.

"Yes?"

"I'm not a writer," he says and clears his throat.

"What do you do?" I ask.

"I'd rather not say," he says. He turns away.

"Oh."

"Have a good day," he says and leaves the room.

What does he not want to say? I wonder. Is he out of work? Is he famous? Regardless, I know that both he and I feel

a hostility that my question precipitated.
Maybe I should have asked, what don't you do?

§

      I notice that every feeling I write about takes place in a certain situation and doesn't last long. The situation doesn't create the feeling, but expresses it. Regardless of what it is, another new feeling quickly takes its place. I'm trying to catch each of them, just for a moment, like fireflies.

§

      I'm walking past a green painted cupola in Palisades Park which has been there as long as I can remember. The park overlooks the Pacific Coast Highway and the ocean. The view of sailboats in the blue water against the clear sky is what a sailboat is all about.
      Twenty-five years ago my son Jules was one year old and we stood by the cupola, tossing a ball back and forth. He was good at catching it with his little hands. But once, I threw the ball and it whizzed past him, bouncing over the top of the cliff. Jules screamed and we ran to the edge. We couldn't see the ball in the overgrowth below. There was no way to get to it. He burst into tears. "I've lost my ball," he said. I picked him up, carried him to the car, and drove along Wilshire toward home. He was inconsolable. When I saw the variety store where I had bought the ball, I stopped and took Jules inside. He was looking at other toys while I bought an identical ball. He didn't see me. Then we continued home. I parked in the

drive, got him out of the car, and at the front door, leaned over to the base of a shrub. I took the ball out of my pocket, dropped it on the ground, and raised up. "Look, Jules!" I said. "It's your ball! It bounced all the way back home!" He was delighted and amazed and relieved.

§

I am going downstairs in the hotel garage to get my car to drive to dinner. The valet car parkers wearing white knit shirts and black trousers run up and down the stairs all day. The concrete is stained. The narrow stairs barely leave room to pass anyone. I'm descending so fast that I almost run into a woman coming from the opposite direction—from the lower garage level. I smile as I pass her, a Chicano woman wearing a blue uniform with a white collar and cuffs. "Hello," I say. "Hello," she answers. She is walking slowly. Obviously she is tired. She works in some capacity in the hotel, but I have never seen her. I turn around after she goes by, just to glance at her. No, I look back because she has hesitated and I wonder why. I watch what she is doing. She sees a piece of trash on a step. She has stopped and is deciding whether or not to pick it up. Then she leans down and does so. There is no question how many things she has cleaned in her life.

§

A neatly dressed woman sits on a counter stool next to me at a popular vegetarian restaurant. I've been talking to a man on my right side who just left. I notice her copper red hair, a sunlight color flattering to her pale, freckled skin. She looks very friendly. At that moment, a man walks up to the counter and tells the waitress he wants a cup of coffee to go. I look at him a minute before I realize that his hands and arms are filthy. His blue jeans and shirt are, too. He is a street person. He gives the redhead beside me a toothy smile. He steps closer in her direction, about to speak. As he does, she raises her palms, warning him away.

"I just want to tell you something," he says, "I won't hurt you."

She shakes her head no, her lips twisted. She looks very frightened. Her hands stay raised.

He takes his cup of coffee, pays, and turns toward the door. He crosses the restaurant and hurries out the entrance. He passes along the glass window, until he is out of sight. I can't see his face.

She takes a deep breath. Her cheeks are flushed; her eyes are almost in tears. "I'm OK," she says, but she is shaking.

"The food is good here," I say.

"Yes," she says. "I come here often." She relaxes, then asks, "What did you order?"

"Vegetable meatloaf," I say. I am glad I have finished already and as I leave, I think about her raised up hand and the man's predicament. She would not talk to him because he was dirty and poor. His condition frightened *her*.

§

The new neighbor next door is playing screaming music that reverberates off my walls and makes the floor of the tenant above him vibrate. I sit in my apartment a few minutes, thinking he will turn down the volume, but he doesn't. Finally, I go into the hallway and knock on his door. I have not met him.

I have seen him once before, a very short, kind of 'cool dude' with a headband and with underwear sticking up several inches from his waistline.

He answers, shirtless, his face unhappy.

"Would you mind turning down your music?" I ask.

"Sure," he says.

"Thanks," I say and leave. When I return to my apartment a moment later, he turns the music up a notch.

I go back into the hallway and knock on his door again.

"I'm not home!" he yells.

I knock. Then again. I hear footsteps. The door opens. Inside I see a clothesline stretched across the room.

"Yes?" he asks.

"I'm trying to work," I explain. "I'm a writer and need quiet."

"I need music," he says.

"Just turn it down so you don't disturb anyone else."

"Why should I? I pay my rent. I write, too. I use my music for inspiration."

"Why don't you get earphones?" I ask.

"I wear them all day at work."

"Don't wear them at work. Wear them at home."

"I have to wear them at work if I listen to music."

"I'll go see the landlord."

"Do that," he says. "I've paid my rent." He shuts the door.

I return to my apartment, but the loud bass and the deafening sound prevents my doing anything other than getting angry.

I go upstairs and knock on the landlord's door. He answers immediately.

"The guy next to me is playing music too loud," I say.

"I know. I have other complaints," he says. "I will take care of it." He walks into the hallway, shuts his door and accompanies me to my apartment. He comes inside. He stands in the middle of the living room. "Yes," he says, "I see." He leaves the apartment and goes next door.

A few minutes later he comes back. "Is this better?"

"Yes," I say. "If he leaves the volume there, that is fine."

"Good," he says, and goes to his apartment.

The next evening, the music is as loud as ever. I stand perfectly still a moment, angry. Then I walk over and knock on the wall.

The tenant knocks back.

I knock.

He knocks.

I go out of my apartment and knock on his door. He ignores me. I knock again. Finally he opens the door.

"Would you mind turning down the music?" I ask.

"Yes, I would," he says. "If it bothers you, move."

"I pay my rent, too."

"So?"

"Look," I say, "I'm trying to get some work done."

"Oh, you're writing a little story," he says. "Big deal."

"What's wrong with you?" I ask. "Why don't you care if you disturb others?"

"It's not my business," he says. "Go away."

"I'll go to the landlord again."

"Good. He says my music is fine."

I leave and go upstairs. The landlord accompanies me downstairs. I go into my apartment.

Several minutes later I answer a knock at the door. It's the landlord and the tenant.

"Can't you just give me two or three hours every night to relax with music?" the tenant asks.

"I pay my rent, too," I say. "And I expect quiet."

"Whenever you knock on the wall," the landlord says, "He'll turn down the volume."

"Good," I say.

"Shake hands and be friends," the landlord says.

The man and I make the gesture. But the loud music has already eradicated any friendship we might have. The apartment remains quiet the rest of the evening.

The next evening when I enter my apartment, music is blasting through the wall. I go over to it. I knock. There is no response. I knock harder. In a few seconds, the volume is raised.

§

The path cutting through Pacific Palisades Park which overlooks the Pacific, is flanked by short grass with ants and tall palms. The palms cast long, skinny shadows. The carefully designed flowerbeds are flourishing. The expanse of the ocean, the mountains, and the park, is sensational, particularly now, at late afternoon.

A well dressed couple walk past where I sit on a

bench. I can overhear their conversation. She is British and I think he must be, too. "*This* is paradise," she says. "Whenever I come to this place, I think of the rain and cold in London. This is paradise if anywhere is."

"Yes," he says, "I agree with you."

They continue ahead and I get up from the bench and walk over to the ledge to look at the view for myself again. Indeed, the view is colored as boldly as any I've seen—even in photographs. The light has a special quality of softness. There is a generosity to it. The water is more blue, and when clouds puff by as they do now, they often are billowy. I look out at the water and at a single sailboat.

But I can't look for long. I catch the beauty in a glimpse. I retreat to the path and the trees. I think that yes, the beauty excites, but there is something about its constancy that can become unsettling. No matter how I feel when I enter the park, it is beautiful. It has glory. It can contrast disheartedly with how I feel inside.

And at times, the view disappears entirely as I pass by it.

§

I am on my way to a meeting in Hollywood and badly need to use the men's room. I pull into the American Burger parking lot off Sunset, go inside, and order an egg muffin to justify my using their toilet. While I wait, I head to the door marked "restrooms" just past the dining area. An older black man seated at a table by the window says, "Someone just went in there."

"Thanks," I say, disappointed and not liking his

warning me. I can find out for myself. I walk back to the counter. The lone cook who is supposed to prepare my food leaves the kitchen, going outside. I see a noisy big truck through the open back door.

Several minutes pass. I walk back into the dining area, cross, open the door and enter the hallway which leads to the bathrooms. I try the door of the Men's. It swings open. I glimpse a man standing at a sink. He is fiercely splashing water onto his hair. I have the impression of a bird in a birdbath. I shut the door quickly. He locks it.

I stand in the hallway in some discomfort. Several minutes pass before it dawns on me that the man is washing himself and not using the toilet at all. He was splashing water all over the floor. Nor does he care if I need to use it. Who does he think he is? I return to the counter to get my order. I keep an eye on the hallway.

It is unbelievable to me how long the man is taking. I decide to try the knob again, just to hurry him. I cross into the dining room.

"There's another restroom," the black man says. "Use it."

"Yes," I say, irritated with him, too. I go into the hallway and try the women's, but it is locked. I go to the men's. After a minute, I return to the empty counter. Has the cook forgotten my order? I wonder.

He is still out back. I take a foam cup from the stack on the counter and walk outside to my car. I sit inside, unzip my pants, urinate into the cup. I pour the piss onto the asphalt as I get out. I throw away the cup in a trash can at the side of the restaurant. I no longer need the restroom.

I go back into the place, happy, see that my egg muffin

is ready, and pay. It smells good. Then I spot the man coming from the hallway. He's in his early twenties, very thin, and has a shaggy beard, long wet hair, and a scrubbed face. He sits at one of the tables. He sets his big pack beside him. Instantly I realize that while I think of the restroom as a place to relieve myself, he thinks of it as a place to clean up. He has no home. It is his refuge.

He gives me a generous, friendly look.

I walk over and hand him a dollar. He seems surprised. He takes the bill. "How are you?" he asks in a very friendly tone like he wants to talk.

I nod.

"What's up?" he asks, his face beaming.

"Not much," I say, and hurry on. I am very glad he is clean. Why was I impatient, I ask myself, when I saw what he was doing?

§

I had no thought of pain when I made the appointment for esoteric acupuncture. The therapist, five feet five or shorter, has kind eyes. First he asked me if I have any physical problem. No. Did I have a spiritual question for him? I hesitated, trying to be polite to this person I did not know. "The acupuncture will enhance your heart chakra," he said.

Now he stands by the bed and shows me the tiny needles he uses. They look longer than tacks. They will sink into my flesh up to one half an inch. I lie back politely, in some horror. He leans over me and begins to push in needles along my chest, at my breast bone (which stings), along my ribs (I think) and in the center of my chin. The needles configure the

Star of David, he says, which I am supposed to picture. I try to. Then he instructs me to visualize light around me, emanating from my crown chakra and flowing into my heart. I should see a lotus which is made of light.

I close my eyes.

He leaves the room.

I am fascinated by the light I perceive, yet am aware of being pinioned by the needles. I am in a kind of prison. I try not to think about it.

Then I open my eyes and notice that he's back in the room. He must have been standing there several minutes. He carries a long horn, about four feet long. He stands back and begins to blow into it. A vibration of air inches from my feet flows up my legs. I close my eyes, aware of the vibration occurring at different parts of my body. The vibration itself is subtle, and the sound is loud. The therapist fades from my awareness. Very drowsy, I feel deep within the experience and he is outside, precipitating it.

The absurdity of the moment makes it more real.

The horn makes a sound like nothing I have ever heard. Like a low moan flowing across a body of water.

I lie perfectly still, hardly aware when he has stopped blowing into the horn. "I'll be back in thirty minutes," he says.

Thirty minutes! I am supposed to lie here thirty minutes with these needles sticking in me? But by the time I have finished the thought I am so relaxed that I can not imagine doing anything else. My awareness of this peace, which is what the experience seems to be, has heightened. Time disappears, most of my body does, as do my thoughts. I am in a simple, trans-experiential state. Random thoughts move across my mind like clouds.

"Hi," he says, touching my arm.

I look up at him.

"The session is over."

I could have been unconscious for all I knew. "Yes," I say. I start to move, then lie back down. I don't know if I have the strength to get up.

"Did you experience anything different?" he asks.

He has a kind of sweet innocence about his face. "We have pathways in our soul," he says. "Where you went was a path that already exists. You can't go any place that is not there." His voice softens. "We have been working on your spiritual muscles. I was glad to help you."

"Yes," I say. To talk about something so personal and unproved with this man who is still unknown to me would embarrass me if not him.

"Make another appointment whenever you like," he says.

"Yes."

He leaves the room. It takes several minutes for me to gather the strength to get up off the mattress. I dress, then walk down the hallway and into the foyer to pay. I give the therapist a tip. Before I leave the place, he comes in.

"Thanks," I say. "That was very peaceful."

"I'll be glad to help you develop more," he says.

When he says this, I feel that he needs the money and that he wants more sessions because of it. I don't think the motivation for what he is doing is monetary (who could make that choice?), but I feel his need. And it is monetary.

Why does he think he can help me spiritually?

"Thanks," I say, as I leave. Wherever I was in my head, I have been before in my meditation, which I had assumed was the most personal thing in the world. But perhaps it was only a place in a mental neighborhood, like a park or a lobby. And I wonder, as I leave and walk down the street, is this man on the path to wisdom, to being a guru? The idea had not crossed my mind before.

§

As I walk along the promenade, an older homeless woman, thin, grey haired, in clean clothes, plants herself directly in front of me, making me stop.

"Can you help me out?" she asks. "My family's hungry."

She is clean and well dressed.

I don't want to give her money because she is confronting me. I am in a hurry. She does not step aside to let me pass.

"Not even a dollar?" she asks.

I smile and walk on. Then I frown and I look a little deeper into myself. I do not want to give this woman money. I realize that I give only when I choose to. Just being asked is not enough.

§

As I enter Elysee Bakery in Westwood, I recognize the wrought iron chairs with orange leatherette seats and small round marble tables from when it opened in 1979. I was its general manager then. Deciding not to try to write for film and in between semesters for college teaching, I oversaw the opening of this and another Elysee at Fox Hills Mall. I picture what it was—smaller, newer, more cozy. They have expanded it. I had great respect for the Iranians who owned it and the franchiser out of Philadelphia. The place had personality. No wonder it has lasted, I think.

The lighting has been changed, but the big French-made oven is in the same place and the original space of the business is very familiar. I want to tell everybody in sight what it was like then and who I was, and how opening the place was exciting.

I walk up to the counter, gazing at the cakes, cookies and muffins. Before opening day in '79 I had called the franchiser and asked how much we should charge for croissants. Almost no one else in LA but us sold them. "Ask the baker, then decide," he said. The baker, who could bake anything, suggested that we charge a nickel or a dime each. Instead, I decided that our initial price was one dollar and seventy-five cents for a plain croissant and two dollars for a ham and cheese.

"Can I help you?" the young man behind the counter asks me.

"I want a napoleon," I say. They look fresh.

"Here or to go?"

"Here, please."

He gets a plastic plate from a stand behind him, turns around, and opens the case for the pastry.

"I opened this place nearly thirty years ago," I say. "I was general manager of two Elysee bakeries then."

He nods.

"It became a success immediately," I say. "I published a short novel about it."

"Huh." He puts the napoleon on the plate and sits it on top of the counter. "What do you want to drink?"

"Just water," I say. "We sold cakes back then that cost five-hundred dollars."

"Bottled or cup?"

"A cup is fine."

He gets a plastic cup.

"Do you like working here?" I ask. I think of the young French couple whom I hired to work the counter. Valentin asked me once if he could give the leftover bread to his French friends. "Of course," I said. We threw away a lot of bread every night. That very afternoon I came into the bakery and every table was occupied. Lots of customers, I thought. Pablo, the night baker, came up to me and whispered. "Valentin is giving everything away. No one is getting charged."

I motioned to Valentin to follow me and took him aside. "Are you giving food away free to your friends?" I asked.

"You said I could give them the left over bread."

"After we close."

"Why wait? If they can have it, then why not have it now? I don't want to give my friends old bread."

"We need the tables for customers. We have to make a profit."

"Profit," he said, like he was spitting.

"You can't give the food out now."

"You want me to ask my friends to leave?"

"Yes."

He stared at me with disdain.

His girlfriend, who had been listening nearby, walked

over. "The croissants," she said, "they are much too big. They should be like so." She measured with her hands. "They are too big. It is vulgar."

"You can give things away after we close, not now."

"Then I quit," he said.

"I quit, too." She untied her apron and marched around the counter toward the door.

They came back the next day.

I pick up the plate with the napoleon and the cup of water. The server doesn't answer my question about his liking working there. He turns around and disappears into the back. He has no interest in my stories. I take a long look around, then carry the pastry and the water to a table.

He wouldn't have a job if I hadn't started the place.

§

Two young Chinese men are taking turns at the lat machine. They lift a lot of weight for their small sizes. They look quite different. One is more handsome than the other. "Excuse me," I say to the shorter one. "Everyone I know believes that in thirty years China will be the most powerful country in the world and the U.S. will lose its place as the only superpower. Do you believe it?"

He hesitates and I look at the other who has stopped working out and is listening happily. Neither is willing to answer. Of course they don't want to offend me. Maybe they don't trust the question.

"It looks reasonable to me, considering our country's problems," I say. "All my friends believe it."

"I do, too," the handsome guy says.

The other nods and smiles.

"Just look at the problems in our country today. When I was a boy everyone thought that the U.S. would dominate the world forever. There was no question of our being number one or of our continued prosperity."

"Yes," one says.

"And now it's China's turn," I say.

"Yes," the handsome one says, then the shorter one nods.

They are understandably proud. "But shouldn't you be living in China and working on your futures there?" I ask.

"We are. We go back and forth. Eventually we will live there again. It will help us to have lived in the U.S."

"Oh," I say. "I'd like to visit China." Then I walk away. So they know what it feels like, being dominant.

That evening I pick up the phone and call my 92 year old mother. During our conversation I ask, "Which country do you think will be number one in twenty-five years?"

"China," she says. "Probably sooner than that."

"Have you ever thought that before?" I ask.

"No," she says. "But it will be."

§

As I walk along the gravel path of the Lake Shrine Center in Pacific Palisades, I know I won't stay long. Just as Palisades Park overlooking the Pacific has spectacular physical beauty, this pond harbors a kind of cultivated peacefulness that I enjoy, but don't want to remain around. It has the loveliness of a place that has been nurtured for fifty-five years by monks and volunteers. The beauty mirrors the quiet emptiness the

Buddhists seek. It makes me think that if I stayed very long, I'd never want to leave.

I begin to walk the path in a quiet, pensive way, paying attention to the flowers and the water and the earth. Imagine so many flowers being planted and cared for. Each nook is inviting, as it is supposed to be. Perhaps the idea of creating the peacefulness is what makes me slightly uneasy. There is not a drop of the naturalness of nature. It is nature made beautiful by how we arrange it.

Nonetheless, the beauty is remarkable—it's a glorious church garden. I am tempted to stop at each of the benches arranged for people to sit or meditate. I choose a white painted wooden bench and sit down.

Being here makes me want to reflect the quiet peace and beauty of the plants and water. It demands appreciation of what has to be innumerable gardeners tending to the place. These ten acres are only a few hundred yards from noisy, busy Sunset Drive.

I close my eyes and get very quiet inside myself. I sit for only a minute or two, aware of a rushing stream behind me. Then I open my eyes.

To my surprise, two women stand very close by. They have stopped walking so that they will not disturb me.

I hide my embarrassment. I smile at both of them.

They begin to walk along the path. As they reach my bench, they stop.

I say nothing, wishing they would go on.

One of the women is overweight and wears a light blue dress. She wears glasses. The other is tall and quite thin, with her hair pulled back into a bun. She has the gracefulness of certain women who naturally move like swans.

The stocky woman eyes me. "Would you pray for us?" she asks.

The other woman has no expression on her face.

The last thing I want to do is to insult them or anyone. Her asking is a kind of compliment, I think. I have come, of course, from a tradition of letting one's own selfish life do its own praying. Kind of a personal statement of faith. And I think that her request is not so different from a homeless person's asking for money. Perhaps that, too, is a kind of compliment.

I nod and close my eyes, more like a frog than a monk.

"Thank you," she says, and walks on. In a minute they are out of my peripheral vision.

I am afraid to get up and leave without praying for them, but I have no idea how and don't want to offend god. I keep my eyes closed, a silent prayer, wordless. I get up and hurry in a different direction along the path, having faced a different kind of garden.

§

The "neighborhood street" outside Versace in Beverly Hills has black wrought iron benches set along the cobblestones. It's built showy for pedestrians, not for cars to drive on. Most of the customers for the expensive stores are tourists and many are foreign. The last string of them passing by where I sit, speak several different languages so that I have trouble distinguishing Italian or Spanish or Portuguese. They are just using sounds as we all do. Oohing and ahhing over the overpriced displays.

A hired man wearing a black top hat and jacket stands at the entrance to this walkway and says, "Welcome to Beverly

Hills. You have arrived."

People hurry past him.

The man beside me on the bench has a lean, long muscular body and face. He appears Slavic but speaks Italian. While I've been sitting here he has been reading endless emails on his blackberry. I haven't leaned over closely enough to read any. His casual clothes are flawless, and his shoes are made of the finest leather.

I'm hesitant as what to ask him about himself. I'm interested in his work, but even more in who he is. So I ask: "Are those e-mails?"

"Yes, they are."

"There are an awful lot."

"I get about 135 a day."

"You read them?"

"It's my job."

"And give people your opinion of things. What do you do?"

"I'm C.E.O. of a company that develops parts for automobiles. I live in Chicago, but I'm from Rome." He hesitates. "I was just thinking that this place is full of tourists."

"Like Disneyland."

"Yes, but it's attractive. Unless you look too close."

"Do you have children?"

"Two. One is three; one is one and a half. A girl and a boy. They're in Rome with my wife."

I nod. "I have a twenty-six year old son getting a Ph.D. Why are you here?"

"I was in a meeting with an investment banker about acquiring a company."

"Oh. How large is it?"

"About one hundred million."

"My goodness. What do you do with it?"

"Merge it with one we own. Get rid of redundancy, use new techniques, and expand sales. Hopefully make money."

"What do you do?" he asks me.

"I run a foundation and write novels," I say. "We give money to novelists. I taught in college many years. But what I really do is interest myself culturally. Where do you live in Chicago?"

"On Lake Michigan. I rent a condo. If you live in Rome you don't get to write off the interest from a mortgage. My neighbor bought his and made two hundred thousand in two years."

"Yes, and you could have."

"Yes. I wish I had."

"But that money is not ours, no matter how much there is of it." I look closer at his face which shows strength and at the same time, kindness. He is a natural leader. His big lips make him rather handsome because of the muscles in his cheeks. His black hair is short. He gives off a confidence that he will be successful no matter what he does. I realize that I enjoy sitting by him.

"I'm thinking I want to live here if we buy the company. In Santa Monica. Or Malibu. I rented a convertible and drove there yesterday."

"You'd like it," I say. "But if you commute, Malibu would be bad because of mud slides."

"Oh, yes?"

"You'd like it out here, though."

"I think so. Living downtown is difficult with two children."

"Imagine yourself fifteen years ago," I say, "You were 22. You didn't know you'd have these things. A great position, financial security, a wife you love, a boy and a girl, good health--. At this moment you have everything."

"Yes," he says, "I feel that I do."

"You really do."

"Yes."

"I mean that whatever else you are doing and no matter what the frustration, you should keep aware of how much you have."

He nods.

"It's a wonderful thing," I say.

"Your situation sounds good, too," he says. "You're here in the middle of the day. You've retired. You have a family. You're a writer. Have you published books?"

"Yes," I say.

"Then you have everything, too."

"Yes."

Both of us look at each other. We smile genuinely, and don't say a word for a minute.

§

The small deli in Beverly Hills has an outdoor seating area, but I sit inside, at a single table by the plate glass window. A tall, well dressed, grey haired man sits beside me. He concentrates on his own thoughts and doesn't look right or left. A newspaper lies on the table in front of him. He clearly minds his own business.

I look down at what he is eating and ask if it is good. His response is non-committal like he does not want to talk.

"It's fine," he finally says.

"What did he order?" I ask the waitress when she comes to the table.

"Ham and cheese quiche."

"I'll take it."

"Yes, with bread or salad?"

"Salad," I say, wondering if I misheard her. Surely bread and salad are not the choices. Soup or salad would be. I choose the vinaigrette dressing.

Then I pull out my notebook. The man picks up a section of the paper and reads it to the end. I get nowhere with what I am doing. I am served, and with the first bite I take, realize why he was not enthusiastic. What could he say? The quiche is like mush. I glance over at him. He obviously is a seasoned professional and minds his own business anyway.

"This quiche is tasteless," I say.

"I know," he says, apologetically. His eyes don't veer toward me even as we talk. He almost looks blind.

"What do you do?" I ask.

"I'm a stockbroker. And I'm seventy."

"What does a seventy-year-old stock broker think about?" I ask.

"About retiring. I've avoided it for several years. But most of my clients are dead."

"Oh, really?"

"Yes. All the most important ones are."

"And do you go get new ones?"

He grins. "Oh, no. I would have years ago. Not anymore."

"Many of my writer friends have died," I say. "I came

here today because a screenwriter friend brought me here once years ago. We sat outside. He lived just down the street on Bedford."

He nods.

"He was a wonderful friend," I say. "We always had a hilarious time—laughing at ourselves and what we were going to do. We talked about going on tour and reading together."

"So you are a writer?"

"Yes."

He says nothing. Years ago almost anyone I told that I was a writer would ask the name of my books. Today everyone tells me about a plot idea they have for writing their book. But he says nothing. I glance at his eyes, which have to have some kind of problem because he is not looking at anything. I wonder who he is and where he lives and what his life is like. Whatever, it must be carefully measured.

"Well, I've been thinking about retiring for a long while," he says. "I just don't know what I'd do all day. Maybe I'll do it next year."

"Yes," I say.

He sighs, then takes the paper and folds it. He looks out the window for several minutes. Then he glances toward but not at me, gets up, picks up the folded paper and walks out of the deli, toward what I guess is his office, and leaves.

I sip from my glass of water. I think of my screenwriter friend whose Academy Award did not make him famous or rich. I remember how funny he was to be around. I can see the table where we ate. Then I think of the man's dead clients. All of these people are still in our lives.

§

I sit on a bench on the Promenade in Santa Monica, talking on the cell phone before I go into the gym. My gym bag is beside me on the bench. I feel a movement, look over, and see that a young guy, with spiked blond hair and wearing a bright pink tee shirt with sequins, is putting his bag beside mine. The suddenness of his action surprises me and to protect my bag and to be polite and give him more room, I scoot mine over. I look up at him.

"I don't want your bag," he says.

"Of course not," I say. "I was just startled." I immediately want to make up for what he thinks is insulting to him.

His voice is mincing and his facial expressions are exaggerated. "Don't talk to me!" he says. He points his finger at me and shakes it. "I hate you! Don't ever speak to me again!" He is screaming; his voice fills the area. He grabs his bag and hurries off, running into a sporting goods store. This happened before I could say anything more.

§

He has an aura of solid compactness and purpose. Wearing a soft blue knit polo and jeans, he sits with a paper cup of gourmet coffee, which he doesn't touch. He will drink the coffee when he is ready. He begins a conversation with me by commenting on the good weather. We are sitting outside at neighboring tables at a coffee place on Ventura Boulevard.

"Yes," I say, "it's real California weather."

"Like Jerusalem," he says. "Dry and sunny."

"Are you from Jerusalem?"

"I lived many years in Israel. I am Jewish."

"But you're an Arab."

"Yes. An Arab and an Israeli Jew. It is not so unusual. I lived there nearly thirty years."

"You were born in Israel?"

There is the slightest crack in his voice. "In Iraq. It is a country of extremes. The minorities hate each other. Not prejudice like in the U.S. In Iraq there is hatred. Sadaam Hussein was very cruel, but he knew how to hold Iraq. Not how to govern. How to hold it in his hands."

He speaks with a definiteness that allows no countering. He does not say what he does not know. He sits erectly, and his gaze is direct. Like an animal on the alert.

"You can't say the same for Bush," I say.

"Yes. But Iraq is an unusual country. If I see a Kurd with a dollar, I take it from him. It is my duty."

"Do you work in Israel?"

"For many years I did."

"What do you do?"

"Security."

"What kind of security?"

"Security," he says. His lips spread into a grin. "It is enough."

"That must be interesting," I say.

"Yes, but sometimes dangerous."

"Oh?"

For over a minute he does not speak. "I have faced my own death many times," he finally says. "I thought, this is it: in one moment I will die. Instead, I reacted and saved myself."

"You thought you were going to be killed?"

"I knew."

"What was that like?" I ask.

"Nothing. It felt like--nothing. I saw it and reacted. Nothing more."

"What do you think about it?"

His hair is short; his dark eyes are focused, narrow. He sees what he looks at. He is handsome, in a manly way, with hairy arms and hair showing at the neck of his shirt. "I don't think," he says. "I don't waste much time thinking. People who think a lot go crazy. They go into circles. But I know people. This woman I meet the other day, she tell me her problems. She blames her boyfriends for breaking up with her, one after another. I tell her what is wrong with her, not them. She says, 'You are right. Are you psychic?' I am not psychic, I say. I know people." He grins. "And I can tell a lot about people by how they walk."

Several people are passing by. I look at how they walk. "Can you really?" I ask.

"Yes. You would be surprised to know how much of yourself you show when you move."

"What kind of danger is involved in your job?"

"Danger is enough. I am not afraid. Once I served on the West Bank. I carried only a knife."

"Oh yes?"

"Many times I have saved my life. My job is no longer dangerous, but it was."

"It sounds like fun," I say. I know my comment is absurd.

He looks at a woman as she passes in front of us.

"She's too young for you," I say.

"No," he says.

"Do you have kids?" I ask.

"I have never been married. I live alone."

"So you've been free?"

"I would be free whether or not I was married. Do you live near here?"

"Yes," I say.

"Why are you here?"

"I've been jogging. I'm 65."

"You do not look 65. You must have heard that many times."

I say nothing.

He looks at me without speaking. Something about him seems truly severe: it is his lack of a sense of irony. The world and he himself are seen in black and white. None of it is funny. War certainly isn't. Nor are other people. Being alive is a serious matter.

"I see very few people," he says. "I stay to myself."

"Yes," I say. "I like your blue shirt."

His smile is relaxed. "I like nice clothes. I have this one in persimmon and in green. I care how my clothes fit. These fat people—people with guts like this (he gestures)— they are repulsive. I eat one meal a day. Whatever I want—I eat a lot. People say, "But you are so skinny and you eat so much."

When he smiles, his mouth opens. I see that his upper back teeth are missing. He must chew with his front teeth.

"I need to lose weight," I say. I finish the bottle of water I am drinking. "I'll see you later," I say, getting up.

"Yes," he says. "Do you come here often?"

"Not often," I say. I nod.

He nods back.

As I leave, I wonder what he can tell about me from how I walk. I don't doubt it's a lot so I try to walk with confidence. In my mind's eyes I can feel his watching me.

About half a block down the street, I turn around to see if he is following me. I have a vague sense of getting shot.

§

"One hope for world peace is the Chinese character," a Chinese man tells me. "In China the Y chromosome is most important. You pass this on to your son and he passes the Y chromosome to his son. Family is of number one importance. But if you are not family, then everyone is treated equally. It is the Chinese way. The minorities who settle in China are assimilated into the population. They do not stay separate and criticize the system.

"Too, the Chinese love America for two reasons. First because after the Boxer revolution, the Americans did not want reparations. Some of that money they spent on establishing a university in China. With the rest they supported Chinese studies at Harvard University. The other reason is George Bush, Senior. When he was Ambassador to China he and his wife would bicycle through the streets of Beijing. The intelligencia saw them and became fond of them. They are very popular in China.

"The Chinese do not want war. Eventually Taiwan will have common goals with China and they will become one democratic country. But the Chinese do have hostility against the Japanese because of how Japan has mistreated China in the past. The militarists are still in Japan and if they regain power,

China would be aggressive and bomb Japan. This situation is one of the sensitive spots in world politics...."

§

The Chicano babysitter laughs with the boys she watches outside Baskin Robbins in Beverly Hills. The children are expensively dressed in warm clothes because the weather is chilly. One boy is about three; the other appears five or six. The three-year-old, laughing really hard, leans back in the white plastic chair while his feet are on the table. He topples over. He hits the back of his head against the sidewalk. A thick knit hat protects him. He stands up, surprised. The woman and the other boy laugh and the young one joins in as he gets up and brushes himself off. He is a good sport. He does not cry.

"Do it again," the babysitter says, "Do it again, Charlie!"

He wobbles into the chair, laughing, puts his feet up on the table and deliberately pushes back again. The chair flips over and he falls, hitting the side of his head and his right shoulder against the concrete walk. "Oh!" he screams.

The babysitter and Charlie's brother burst into laughter.

"Do it again!" she says. "Come on, do it again!"

He stands up and rubs his head. "I'm not going to do it again," he says. "It hurts." He tries not to cry.

"It's so funny," she says. "Do it again!"

He sits down quietly.

"There's mama," the older son says. The babysitter sits up straight. She begins to stack their dishes.

Mother is dressed like a window display in a fancy

store. She is rail-thin, with long blonde hair. Her lipstick is perfectly drawn on her lips which pooch. She is in a hurry. "Let's go," she says. "Come on. Come on." She bends down to Charlie. "Hello, sweetie," she says in a loving tone.

He reaches up to kiss her.

"Now put your napkins into the trash," Mother says. "It's bad to litter."

Charlie walks to the container and drops in the napkin and cup. "I fell over in my chair," he says.

"He didn't hurt himself," the babysitter says. "And we ate coconut ice cream. It was so good." She swipes the outdoor table with her napkin.

"I hope it's not too much sugar," Mother says. "Hurry up. We're going to the car." She puts her arm around her older son.

They rush off with Charlie rubbing the side of his head. The babysitter walks behind Charlie. She reaches up and straightens his cap.

§

Stopped at a red light, in my white convertible with the top down, I hear someone in the next car shouting toward me. I turn to him.

"Can you multi-task?" he asks. He's got long brown hair, a mustache, is thin and about thirty. His pick-up is customized and silver with expensive exhaust pipes.

"Yes," I say.

"Do you have a cell phone?"

"Yes." The noise of the traffic is almost deafening.

"Will you call my doctor? I'm late for an

appointment."

"Sure. What's the number?" I ask. This is what we all need in traffic—something to do.

The light changes before I get the number. We move along. He shoots ahead and I press on the gas to keep up. At the next light, we are across from each other again. He yells above the sound of motors: "310-555-5555. Dr. Osner."

"How do you spell it?"

"Just call him."

"What's your name?" This light switches to green. A driver in the car behind honks. I can't very well explain he's late if I don't know his name. I hang up, keeping alongside.

"Harry Norman," he says when we stop. "Can you hear me?"

"N-o-r-m-a-n?"

"Yes. Thanks!"

I dial the number and after several rings, get a doctor's office. "I'm calling for Harry Norman," I say. "He's on his way."

"It's good you called. I was about to cancel him," the receptionist says.

"Please don't. He's coming."

"All right."

"Thank you," I tell her and hang up. I call out: "Okay. I got them."

The cars are noisier than ever. I am ready to pull out. "What's your name?" he asks.

"Jim."

"Glad to meet you. I'm from South Africa. Where do you live?"

"Santa Monica." I suddenly discern a slight accent in

his English.

"Let's get a beer sometime. What's your email?"

The light changes. We drive to the next light. He raises his hand—he has a pen and paper. He writes down my email as I shout it out.

"That's too fast," he says. "Again."

I repeat it.

"I've got it," he says. "I'll email. Thanks." He waves.

"Sure," I say, as his truck zooms away at the corner where I am about to turn left. For some reason, I hope he emails me.

§

The homeless man I pass as I am about to walk into the bank foyer to use the ATM makes his voice pathetic as he asks for money. I hand him a dollar and he leaves. Inside the foyer, I insert my card, then press in the code. I make the various selections to get cash. I can't help but feel guilty. Should I be responsible for others' welfare on some level— even if it's only caring?

As the money spits out, a black guy is punching in his secret access code on the machine next to me. Then he punches in the amount. His money soon shoots out. We both watch it. He takes it, as I did mine.

I turn to face him.

"Did you get twenties?" I ask.

"Yes," he says.

"Hey," I say, excited. "Can we do something? Can I give you five of mine and you give me five of yours?" I hold mine up. "This way we're at least sharing. It seems less selfish."

"I can do that," he says.

I count out the hundred. "Here," I say.

He takes the bills and counts out a hundred dollars for me. Both of us are laughing.

"Don't you feel better?" I ask. "You have my hundred; I have yours."

"Somehow I do," he says. "I don't know why."

"I do, too," I say. "Thanks." Then we both turn around and leave the foyer. Who says sharing has to be giving something away, I wonder.

§

Leaving my apartment, I go along the outside walkway and out the metal grill to the alley. Immediately ahead I see a woman about my age digging into the trash. I walk past, glancing at her. She ignores me. Her grey hair is matted; her skin is dirty, too. She has to be in her sixties like me.

After a few steps I turn around and walk up to her. I hand her a five dollar bill that I have just taken from my pocket. "Here," I say.

She reaches out and takes it. She looks at it. "Wait a minute," she says.

I am just walking off. I turn back. "Yes?"

"Why did you give this to me?"

I am startled, defensive. "Because…" I don't want to insult her. "I thought you were homeless."

"I am. But why did you give it to me?"

"I thought you needed it?"

"But why give it?" Her expression is very serious. She

holds the money like she may give it back.

"Because I care about you," I say.

She breaks into a full smile. "Thank you, then," she says.

§

Standing in line in front of me is a dark haired woman holding a fluffy dog. The yogurt shop is mobbed with children. I feel as if I can hardly wait another minute in line, having driven across Los Angeles in traffic. I consider leaving the store.

The dark haired woman turns to me. "Don't you like this dog?" she asks. She is holding a small, curly haired dog. "She's a special dog. Let me give you her card." She reaches into her purse and brings out a card with the dog's picture, an email, phone, and information about what the dog does. "She works in hospitals with children and with the elderly."

"What does she do?" I ask.

"She's very loving, very special. People love her. She can help heal them."

I pet the dog. The dog doesn't seem very happy. The woman reaches down and kisses it on the mouth. "Sweetie," she says. Whatever else, the dog has worked her magic on the woman.

"She puts people in good moods, too," she says.

I pet the dog again, wondering if that will calm me down. Give me some patience. I look the dog in the eye, but she looks away.

"Yes," she's a nice dog," I say.

I wonder if it is right to put this responsibility on a

dog. Of course they help us. But should we put them to work? Make them earn their keep?

§

I've been riding forty-five minutes on a bus to downtown and can't tell if anyone around me is feeling much. The heavy woman to my right coughs repeatedly. She has a pink and blue nylon bow on the top of her hair, which is pulled into a bun. She is very heavy, 50, and wears a short white skirt and halter. The guy to my left sleeps. He has asked me to wake him up when we get to McArthur Park. A birthmark covers half of his face. He is heavily freckled. His black hair is dirty under his baseball cap. He says he slept on the beach and is from Boston. "If you go downtown," he tells me, "don't go off Broadway."

"Why?" I ask.

"All kinds of things happen there."

"Are you going back to Philadelphia?" I ask.

"I want to," he says but with no resolution. "I'm going to the social security office."

He gets quiet and goes to sleep. Everyone on the bus is in the pull of wanting, the traffic slowly moving, and the air conditioning too cold. The stops are endless.

§

Downtown, off Broadway, a number of streets are crowded with addicts, homeless, and other sub social types. Most of these are black. Many sit or lie on flattened cardboard boxes. There are several thousand, it appears.

Being the only white to walk along these streets at the moment, I notice more than I would otherwise. While I don't look in anyone's eyes, I see them clearly.

I pass a surprising number of strong, good looking men. Something other than being big and handsome has brought them to this state. I get the feeling that while there is a kind of liberation here, almost no one chooses to be a part of it.

They are aware of me, too. A couple of men make a slight gesture for me to stop and talk, but I don't.

After walking several blocks and realizing I am the only white person I have seen, I feel a slight discomfort. It is not enough to make me turn back.

Instead, I sit down on the pavement beside two older guys who ignore me. A minute later a shirtless, light skinned, muscled guy comes up. "I can get anything you want," he says.

"Like what?"

"Cocaine, marijuana, heroin, liquor, wine, beer, sex scenes. Just name it."

I pull a dollar from my pocket. "I want to see your tattoos," I say. "Ok?"

His face is proud. "Sure," he says and moves up close. He stands still.

What strikes me are the tattoos across his nose and down to his lips, across his forehead, and curling around his neck. His chest is a vast pictorial of a romantic scene with dragons and his back is a showcase of a medieval knight. The faces of women and men are clear, well done. His tattoos are professional. None are homemade.

I am afraid to keep his attention too long. "Beautiful," I say. "They're beautiful."

"Thank you," he says. "Get in touch with me if you need anything. And I mean anything. I'm always here. On this block."

"Thanks," I say.

He walks off. I sit a few minutes, the sidewalk comfortable if dirty.

I soon get tired of watching everything around me as if it isn't safe. I don't feel the slightest threat.

Nothing happens in the next half hour. Guys walk past, greeting others on the sidewalk.

Finally I get up and walk across the street to the bus stop. I see a bus coming. Just as it arrives, one of the homeless walks over to me and puts a token in my palm. "Here," he says, "this way you don't have to pay."

I thank him and he leaves. Then I get on the bus and in no time am out of the world where they live day and night.

§

The young man who sits by me wants to talk. I can tell because I do, too.

We glance at each other a few times and finally I ask, "Are you a student?"

"I just graduated from UCLA," he says.

"What did you study?"

"Psychology and English."

"Good subjects," I say.

"Not really. They don't prepare you for anything specific."

"They make you more capable in your head."

"I don't think so," he says with confidence. "The

classes were mostly boring. What we read was not relevant to getting a job. I had TA's most of the time. At a big state university, you don't get to know professors."

"It's a famous university."

"I don't know what a college education is good for now. You study things from other eras."

I nod. Discussing that would require more time than we have and lead nowhere.

"I wouldn't do it again," he says.

"You have to have an education to get a good job," I say. "Education is very important."

"I'm going to start my own business," he says. "I don't need a degree to do that."

"UCLA is very beautiful," I say.

"Is it?"

"It has that reputation. Of course with the huge medical complex, it's harder to park and get around." I remember when Westwood was a village and parking around UCLA was plentiful.

"I don't want to sound negative," he says. "I'm telling you the truth."

"Yes," I say. I wonder what happened in his education to make him feel jaded already. How would I feel if I were an undergraduate now. We certainly never thought of tying our studies to finding a job. He reminds me of the Narodnicks in Russian history. It
would be hard to know what to believe in if I were his age.

§

I'm eating turkey and dressing at Clifton's Cafeteria in downtown LA. The women in line behind me as we chose our food said they come here to eat it every chance they get. I can see why. The tender meat is succulent. The mound of dressing is set next to the potatoes and cranberries.

A Chicano woman in an orange dress sits down at the table closest to mine. She wears a hat and carries her purse and a plastic sack with purchases. Her face is ultra bright with make-up.

She, too, has selected turkey and dressing. She also has a small green salad and mashed potatoes. She takes the hot sauce bottle from the center of the table, opens the top and shakes it over her food, drowning hot sauce on the turkey and dressing. She begins to eat.

I do, too.

She coughs. Then she coughs again. "It's too hot," she says aloud to no one. She waves her fingers in front of her lips. Then she gets up, goes to the trouble to take her jacket which she has put on the back of the chair, her sack, and her purse. She hurries toward the serving counter. A minute later she returns with a glass of water. She drinks from it as she sits.

Then she takes a bite, coughs, fans her fingers over her lips and takes another sip.

She has overdone the hot sauce.

I finish eating and go to the bathroom downstairs. As I return, her table is in my direct view. She waves her fingers fast, her eyes pleasant, and she coughs. Then she sees me, waves, and smiles, like she knows that I know what she has done.

I smile back; it is our private joke. I wave and smile back at her.

§

The flyer posted outside the hotel in downtown LA says the rooms are $300.00 a month. I open the glass door and walk inside, past signs stating that no visitors are allowed, no food can be brought to the room and no loud music is permitted. Nor can you smoke. The manager's office is just off the foyer.

He looks up very confidently.

"Can I see a room?" I ask.

"Of course you can," he says. He gets up, holding a bundle of keys, locks the office, and steps into the hallway.

"Let me show you this," he says. He walks me into a large communal kitchen.

"You can cook here all you want. But no hot plates or cooking is allowed in the rooms."

"Yes," I say. "Is it safe here?"

He grins. "Is the Pentagon safe? Is the White House? Is Beverly Hills? I don't know how to answer that question."

"You're right," I say as we leave the kitchen and walk to the elevator. We get on then get off on the second floor, continue a short way down the clean hall and he unlocks a room. "Come in," he says.

I am surprised that someone has chosen to paint the walls a shocking pink. The tiny room has a half bed, a bureau, a table and two plastic chairs. The furniture is depressing. But the place is very clean.

"Look in the bath," he says.

I step into the bath, aware he's watching. The thin linoleum is pulling up at the edges. The commode looks well used. The shower has a thin curtain and there is a small sink with rusty chrome handles.

"Thanks," I say. "I'm looking around at places."

"If you leave now it means you aren't interested. Sit down on the bed. Stay a while." His voice is an order.

He doesn't really know I was just curious and not looking for a place when I asked to see a room. I feel obligated to give him time since I took up his. I sit on the bed, which has no box springs, only a thin mattress that curls up around me. I look toward the window. There is a view of a brick wall. I could not imagine living in such a place.

"What do you think?" he asks.

"Yes," I say. "It looks fine. I will be back in touch." I stand up and he does not protest.

He follows me out.

"There is a twenty-five dollar fee to apply. If you are denied credit, we keep the money. If you are accepted, we charge it as a processing fee."

"Yes."

"You have to have a job to prove you can pay the rent for six months. There's a six months lease."

"I'm retired," I say.

"Good for you," he says. "You still have to prove you have the income."

We get on the elevator, neither of us speaking. I have disappointed him. We get off on the first floor.

"Thanks," I say. We have reached the foyer where I entered.

"Take a flyer," he says. "It has all the information. And

did I say that no visitors are allowed in the rooms."

"Yes," I say. "Thanks."

He turns around and goes back into his office.

§

A bearded young man sits on the grass in the park, chanting. The pace is manic, like he has autism. He wears a wool toboggan over his thick dark hair. His shirt and pants are black. I sit not far away, reading. At first I enjoy his chanting, but it soon begins to get on my nerves. I can't quite distinguish the sounds.

It becomes irritating.

See how long you can stand it, I tell myself. Don't get up and leave. My stomach tightens as I listen. Is this a religious verse or gibberish?

Listening closely, I hear: "Disopitch...disopitch... disopitch...disopitch." I try not to be too obvious. I look down at my book.

He raises his voice and suddenly I understand his words: "Die son of a bitch, die son of a bitch, die son of a bitch." He is not talking to me exclusively, but he shouts it out anyway. He is addressing the world. He is repeating it thousands of times.

A shaved head bully, homeless, with a girlfriend, sits on the other side of the sidewalk. Finally, the shaved head yells to the chanter: "What did you call me?"

I instantly think that the chanter is not responsible for the chant: he is expressing his experience in the world. He is hurt. He slows chanting, then stops for a moment. He starts again. He can not stop.

"Don't call me a 'bitch'," the shaved head screams. His voice is as threatening as his muscles.

And isn't the chanter chanting to himself anyway? I think.

A moment later, the shaved head begins to mimic the chanting.

The chanting stops. The man chanting begins to gather his belongings.

The shaved head pulls his shirt off over his head. His muscular body is covered with tattoos. One large one on his leg depicts rain—or tears. Tattoos cover the small of his back, his legs, his biceps. He glances over at me. I turn away.

The chanter stands up. He resumes his chanting as he walks away.

"What did you call me?" The shaved head asks. He gets up too and hurries after him. "You'd better watch your tongue."

The chanter stops. The afternoon is suddenly quiet, at least for a moment, then the chanter walks quietly away, further toward the pier. The shaved head flexes his muscles and looks again at me, a scowl on his face.

I turn away, but he has shown me his hurt, too.

§

The film I'm watching at West Side Pavilion is not all that interesting, but a ringing cell phone blares in the row behind me. I glance back, aware of how embarrassed the woman must be. But she does not turn it off. She bends over, her hands cupped around the speaker. "Hello?" she says, "what?" She is having trouble hearing because of the noise of the film. "Lynda?" She hesitates. "I'm so glad you caught me."

Someone in the theater shushes her. "I can't hear," she says.

She doesn't feel the slightest responsibility to shut off the phone because she would miss her call. How interesting, I think, that everyone else in the theater feels a silent responsibility to follow the instructions—the warnings—we are given on the screen. Watch out, or you'll disturb others. This censorship means nothing to her.

"Hello?" she repeats. She sits up straight. "I can hear you now. Would you keep Austin tonight?" She speaks in a normal voice. "Yes. Anytime you can come. I do appreciate it. I have to get off the phone because I'm in a movie. Bye."

She turns off the phone, puts it into her purse, then focuses on the screen again. I face the screen.

What should we expect, I think, having phones to carry anywhere.

The man next to me is looking at her, too. No one else says a word of protest, and it's already too late anyway. What difference would it make?

It takes several moments for people around her to focus on the film. Afterward, as we are getting out of our seats and lining up to leave, I make sure to get a good look at her like she is some kind of criminal.

§

This afternoon in Palisades Park is as glorious as the one before it. Strollers follow the paths and look out at the view. The blue of the sky is as calming as the expanse of water. The sun makes distinct shadows of the palms, on the thick, healthy grass. I'm about to start a slow thirty minute jog. Somehow all these people enjoying the park, day after day, are strangers. I never know anyone or want to. I am a stranger as they are. This not knowing each other is a kind of privacy.

I watch a woman pull up into a parking slot, stop her car, kill the engine, and get out. She hurries. She is headed for someplace. She rushes over to a Eucalyptus tree, and ignoring us, wraps her arms around its trunk. Her hands pat the bark as her arms caress the trunk. Her eyes are closed. And she had hurried from her car because something about the tree had drawn her.

I wonder what she would do if I walked over and asked her to hug me. Then I ask myself, why don't I hug trees? Even worse, I dislike her hugging them. Yet I'd probably prefer hugging the tree to hugging her.

If Theresa of Avila in her brilliant *Autobiography* can write convincingly about walking into a garden and seeing rocks breathing, why do I look askance at this woman hugging this lovely (and maybe lonely) tree? Would I care if she did it in private?

§

When I think of what to write about my experiences yesterday, nothing comes to mind. Could I have paid so little attention to what was going on? I walked past thousands of people without noticing what any felt. I met individually with others and time passed.

The cashier at Kmart when I purchased a dish rack and stainless steel pan was tall and chunky, almost too big to work behind the counter. There was a long line of customers in a hurry behind me. He seemed uneasy.

"You're busy," I said, thinking he must be twenty-four or twenty-five. (The difference would matter to him.)

"Yes," he said. Then he glanced directly at me. "It goes faster that way."

"Yes," I said. I knew exactly what he meant—that on the surface, his time spent doing what he did not want, went faster. He put his finger on how we spend most of our lives—driving on the highway, watching TV, getting places, not listening to people, eating in a hurry, making endless talk on the phone and in person, and telling ourselves we want what we don't. My buying the dish rack was just as wasteful of time as was his standing on his feet making a few dollars.

§

That evening I went to meditation and afterward, two of the four people present talked about their projects. The man had written a book he was self-publishing and wanted to promote and sell. The woman had made beautiful art jewelry she hoped galleries would display. Their time was well spent doing these projects, but now each was more than ready to involve the time of other people—which was an intention of their projects all along.

We think of each day as belonging to us, yet we spend most of the twenty-four hours taking up the time of other people. We depend on their time to take care of our wants. If we are not careful, there will be no time left for anyone, because they depend on our time to take care of their wants, too.

Later, as I walked along Palisades Park back to my apartment, a homeless older black man asked me for a dollar, which I gave him. He reached over instantly and grabbed my hand. He squeezed and held it, then he looked me eye to eye—his eyes widening like a witch doctor's—and brought his cheek so close it almost touched mine. "I love you," he said. What he meant was that he was happy to get the money. He loved what it could buy. Luckily, he was spared idiosyncrasies of my personality which would drive him up the wall. He only had to deal with my generosity and my desire to please others.

We have a sensitivity within us that can take the time we waste each day, and by paying attention to it later, allow us to suddenly notice what we saw and felt. The details of our day submerge and surface—and our feelings are within them.

Writing about our experiences means noticing the details.

§

I am exercising my biceps. Next will come triceps. Using the pulleys, I lift one arm at a time using as much weight as I can. On the other side of the machine, a young balding guy is working out his triceps. I focus on my workout, lifting until my arms are tight.

Then I go over to the triceps pulley the young man has been using. Without checking the weight, I pull down—or try to lower the bar. It doesn't budge. He lifted it easily and I may as well be trying to lift a thousand pounds. He was much stronger than I realized. I take off weight and continue with my triceps.

Then I use the elliptical machine for half an hour.

When I walk into the dressing room, I see the young man in a white shirt and tie, about to leave to go back to work. I go to my locker.

"You lift a lot of weight on triceps," I say to him.

He stops, look over surprised and asks, "What?"

"I couldn't budge it."

"I just do a few exercises," he says. "I need to do more."

"You're strong. I thought I could lift it, but I didn't come close."

"I only do two or three exercises," he says. "I really need to do more."

"No you don't," I say. "You're fine. That was a lot of weight."

He is smiling. He turns around to leave the locker room. Then he faces me again. "Hey," he says, "I just want to say thanks for the compliment. I needed it."

"Sure," I say. I hadn't meant expressly to compliment him. I was stating fact. I think that my telling him was partly a complaint—not that it's his fault. Maybe I was reminding god that he made this guy stronger than me. Being shorter and weaker has to be compensated for.

I am glad I made the guy feel good. That makes me feel good.

§

His face is one piece, smooth, his head shaved, his eyes narrow. He is Tibetan and reading fortunes by examining one's face. I agree to a price and sit on a folding chair across from him. He spreads his hands, across my forehead, then his fingers trace up and down, his eyes close to mine.

I expect nothing, of course.

He begins to talk: "Your eyes and nose are open wherever you go," he says. "You are easy in most situations. You do not have to worry about money. If you need a hundred dollars, a hundred dollars comes; if you need a thousand, a thousand comes. Sometimes you worry too much—like a screwdriver is turning on each side of your head. You can make half a heart with one hand or finger, never a whole heart. It takes another hand or finger to make a whole heart. Like this. He shows me.

"You do not care about going one way. You can go this way or that way. It does not matter. You accept; you go on, you smile. You are too smart. I am sure serious. You are too smart. You will live a long life. No real problems. A good life."

"Where did you grow up?" I ask.

"In Tibet."

"Where?"

"In a temple from age one to ten. My father had three girls and three boys. He did not make much money. He could not afford to keep me. The monk asked for me and I asked my mother if I should go to the temple with the monk and she said, yes, of course. I will be proud, she told me. I went to the temple to live. Every day I meditated, I chanted, I cleaned the floors. Every day for ten years."

"Then you left?"

"It is not my whole life, I tell them. I promise to come back every year for the rest of my life and I do. I go every year."

"Was the monk upset you left?"

"No. It is your life," he said.

"Your face," he continues, "is like mine. You and I are much alike. I feel someone coming into your life, someone soon."

"Yes," I say.

"It is so," he says. "You will see."

A girl walks up and looks at the bracelets for sale on the table. "Mine like this has stretched," she says. "How much are these?"

"I will fix yours," he says. He takes the bracelet, cuts it with pliers and begins to restring it. "One minute," he says to me. "Okay?"

"Yes," I say. I look at the girl and her boyfriend who stands beside her.

The fortune teller finishes the bracelet. "Thank you," he says.

"How much?" she asks.

"No charge. No. No. It is a pleasure, for you."

"How old are you?" I ask her.

"Sixteen. My boyfriend is seventeen."

"I'm from Seattle," he says. He is tall, very innocent.

"I've been there," I say.

"I love it," he says. "You know it?"

"I like it."

He smiles happily. "It is my home."

"Thank you," she says to the Tibetan.

He is smiling, too. "Let's talk," he says to me.

"Tell me about the temple," I say.

"There is a temple inside us. And a temple our bodies live in. In temples today, 80% of the monks live inside the temple but outside of themselves. Will you meditate with me? A minute or two?"

"Yes," I say.

He shows me how I should hold my hands. We meditate several minutes. Then he reaches over and pats my ribs. "Pat them every day," he says. "It is good for your heart. Your life is OK. It is a good life. Go with peace."

§

The man sitting across from me is 6'2" and weighs 255 pounds. He lifts over 700 pounds and looks like he can, all muscle. When I ask him what it's like to lift 700 pounds, he says it looks much harder to do than it is. "If you can do it," he says, "it is not hard."

"Yes," I say.

"I will lift a lot more."

He's eating blueberry pancakes because he's just finished a long workout.

"What's it like to be so big?"

"I don't feel big," he says. "This is me. Lots of guys are bigger than I am."

"I'd be mean if I were big," I say.

"Naw," he says. "But I don't feel big."

"Well, you are."

He went to an Ivy League school and studied philosophy. He works in engineering.

"Terrible about the hurricane hitting Biloxi," he says. "I used to gamble there. We went nearly every weekend."

"They'll have to rebuild it," I say.

"It was ugly—with lots of rednecks. Woman with fat bellies and mini skirts."

"How much would you win?"

81

"About 2500. Not bad for a weekend."

"What do you do?" he asks.

"A retired teacher and a writer."

"I am thinking of changing," he says. "I've made several real estate deals. I'm thinking of the mortgage industry."

"What did you plan to do with the philosophy?"

"I never wanted the academic. My father was a department chair in a college. That's ruthless."

"Yes, it is. You've done a lot of things to be so young."

"I'm 33. Not so young. I worked in Europe for a year. That was interesting."

"What would you really like to do?"

"Go to the top in weightlifting. I have a couple of years left. I don't really care about money. There's only so much you can do with it. I blew out a quadriceps a couple of years ago. A guy working out nearby said he saw it just pop out. I didn't know what happened."

"What did you do?"

"I went into Judo. But that's a rough sport. You can hurt your back from the throws."

His phone rings. He answers it. "Yeah, I'm on my way," he says. "Five minutes." He stands up, his face lighted. "Do you eat here often?" he asks.

"Sometimes," I say.

"I'll see you again," he says and leaves through the glass door nearby.

§

"My dad was a hippie," Chad says. "So when I was in high school he told me to experiment with drugs. "Go ahead," he said. "Get it out of your system." I started with pot and worked my way up to heroin. I didn't tell my parents until two years ago that I do heroin. They got upset of course. I worry about how they worry about me. My brother found me the other day at this coffee shop. He said that my parents are afraid I'll kill myself. But I don't want to die. I want to live. I just want to change my life.

"I took a hit about an hour ago. That's why I was so drowsy when you came up. But I can't sleep long. Once when I was in detox I didn't sleep for longer than ten or fifteen minutes for three weeks. It makes you crazy. My eyes crossed and I went to the doctor. I saw everything double. He told me it would be OK, and it was, but I was frightened."

Chad has long blonde hair and blue eyes. He's short, thin, with arms that if you look closely are scarred from taking hits. A couple of places show where a vein collapsed. He says that when a nurse tries to take his blood she can't find a vein, but he never has trouble. He uses needles for diabetics. He looks like a preppy. His clothes are clean. He's handsome.

"What's it like to take heroin?" I ask.

"I'd get high at first, but I don't anymore. I take it to keep from feeling bad. If I don't I'll start vomiting and break out in fever. Then I feel so bad I can't describe it. I'll do anything to keep from feeling like that. I've been to rehab many times. I just got out a month ago. They kicked me out because I tested dirty. I had to wait a month to reapply. I'm hoping to go back on Monday. My friend and I both have applied."

"Where's the rehab?"

"One is a few blocks from here, but they won't take me back. I'm hoping for a place in the valley."

"You just take a bus there and check yourself in?"

"Yeah. A woman from the other place is my friend. She's trying to help me. I check with her on Monday. Until then I don't want to feel sick. So I have to shoot up."

"How often?"

"Two or three times a day."

"How much does it cost?"

"Twenty dollars a hit. Sometimes more. It depends on what it's like. I've waked up before with IV's connected all over me because I OD'd."

"Where?"

"The last time was in the bathroom of a coffee shop. I took a hit, then a little more. For some reason I took all I had. I almost died. It was stupid."

"What did that feel like?"

"Well, I was with my great uncle. He was taking me to the hospital to detox. I realized on the way that I had some left. So when he stopped the car I ran across the parking lot to a pizza place and into their bathroom. I locked the door and took all of the heroin. When my cousin realized what was happening, he ran into the pizza place and when I didn't answer, he kicked down the door. They took me to the hospital. I passed out. I don't know what it feels like exactly to OD. It doesn't feel like anything."

"Then why do you keep taking it?" "I don't want to be sick again. Once I was in a rehab that had us in a sauna five hours a day. We'd surf, then we'd go into the sauna, then surf, then go back in."

"Usually it's cold turkey?"

"I've gone cold turkey several times. I will next week."

"How about methadone?"

"It's a drug, too. I don't want that shit. I want to get my life back in order. I'm behind. I want to get back in school, graduate, then get a master's."

"Did you know that the average college undergraduate is 27? You're 24. If you go back to school in a year, you're still ahead."

"I thought maybe you were a cop," he says. "Or that my parents sent you."

"No," I say. "So where do you sleep?"

"In an abandoned home with a friend. My blanket is there, and my bike. It gets real cold. This morning some Mexicans found us and were OK, then when the white guys came to work they gave us shit. They said we couldn't stay there. But sleeping on the beach is too cold. And it's dangerous."

"Where do you get the heroin?"

"Anywhere. It's all around, man."

"Where do you get the money?"

"Robbing stores. My friend and I go into one and he distracts them. This morning I had a stack of CD's and looked over at someone at the counter. He was watching. He shrugged; he didn't care. I put another handful in my pack. We take them to other stores and sell them for two or three dollars each. Every night I worry about how I'm going to get the money for the next hit. I hate robbing. I'd never rob a person. For several years I had a job. I kept getting cash advances. I messed up my own shit. I never robbed. I had my own desk, a file cabinet with keys. A phone."

"It's good you are going into rehab."

"And I've still got my teeth. I don't look wasted like so many."

"You will if you don't stop."

"Yeah. God I hope they let me in soon. I'm afraid I'll get put in jail for robbing and have to go cold turkey in jail. That'd be hell."

"Yes, it would."

"Can I have your number?" he asks. "So I can call you in rehab? Your friends never come. Only family. I can talk to you. I'd like to talk to you again."

"Sure," I say and give him my number. Then I give him twenty dollars.

§

The phone rings at 8 a.m. I am still asleep. I answer on the eighth or ninth ring. It's Chad. "Can we meet?" he asks.

"Of course not," I say. "I have to work. Where are you?"

"I'm feeling sick. I'm going to Hollywood to buy heroin. When can we get together?"

"Call me at six," I say.

I think about him off and on all day, this young man hurtling around Hollywood, possibly stealing in order to buy heroin. Twenty-four hours before it wouldn't have seemed possible. I feel obligated to meet him if I can, but won't give him more money. Just before six I arrive at a coffee shop in Venice. My cell rings five minutes later.

"Can we talk?" he asks.

"Sure." I tell him where I am.

Twenty minutes later he shows up, wearing a fresh shirt. When he goes to sit down, I ask, "Are you hungry?"

"I haven't eaten since yesterday," he says. "Sure."

"Let's go eat," I say. We leave the building and are walking along Main Street in Venice. "What kind of food do you want?"

"Whatever you want," he says.

"No, you choose."

"I don't care."

"All right." I turn into the first café. "Is this okay?"

"Sure." We order water to drink and hold the menus. A few minutes later we order stir fry for me, spaghetti for him. "Was your mother a good cook?" I ask.

"She is a great cook. The best food I ever had. She cooks this one dish—it's chicken with a light sauce. She roasts the vegetables with it. She was born in France, in Rouen."

"Lucky you," I say. "How was your day?"

"I go to detox tomorrow afternoon."

"And what do they do there?"

"They check me in and give me medicines to counter going off the heroin. Something to keep me from having a stroke, something for my stomach, and others. Every morning you get your meds. You get them four times a day. They'll give me a cot with sheets and a blanket and a pillow. That's the best part—three meals a day and a place to stay."

"And then you move to rehab?"

"It is a rehab. It detoxes you first. Other places don't. I'll be off the heroin in seven or eight days. I've never stayed in rehab over a month. This time I want to stay as long as I can. I want to get my head straight."

"Yes," I say. He doesn't look good. His eyes have a kind of dead look, and his complexion is dull. "Did you shoot up today?"

"Of course. Or I'd be sick now."

"Where?"

"Here," he says, showing me a place on his arm. It's one of several lumpy looking spots if you look closely.

"Where did you do it?"

"A coffee shop."

"How did you buy it?"

"Just called someone and he came in a car to where I was. Took him about five minutes. I gave him twenty dollars."

"Did you have to go to Hollywood? I heard heroin is only five dollars downtown."

"That's weak stuff. It wouldn't phase me. The guy I call here wouldn't come. He said not to call him anymore. I've been shortchanging him. If I buy thirty dollars worth I'll give him twenty-six. Or if it's fifty, I give him forty-two. So he's pissed off."

"You bought it then went into a coffee shop, into the restaurant and just took a hit? Then you felt good."

"Not good. I felt okay. I don't get high anymore. I'm just trying not to feel bad. But I don't feel good."

"How many did you take?"

"Two. I have a little bit left."

"It's in your pocket?"

"Yep."

"With your syringe?"

"Yes. And a spoon I made from the top of a can."

"How do you make the spoon?"

"Just twist it off and shape a little handle. I'll show you later."

"Thanks," I say to the waitress who brings the dishes of food. I reach across and taste his pasta first. It's good.

"You know eating with you is the first time in two years I've sat down with someone."

"Who are your friends?" I ask. "You can't have any, can you?"

"No." He takes his first bite. "You're my only friend right now," he says.

"Do you have a girlfriend?"

"Heroin. It's my girlfriend. I don't have a sex drive when I'm on it. With my last girlfriend, I could have sex, but it didn't mean anything. When I get clean the drive will come back."

"It's controlling everything in your life."

"Yes. Every day I hunt the money to buy the stuff so I don't feel sick. Then every night I worry about getting the money to buy enough for the next day. I feel bad about my parents. I know they worry about me all the time. But I can't call them because they will know I'm not telling the truth. I'll call them every day from rehab. They'll be glad about that."

"Can you eat okay?"

"Yeah, I'm okay. I've had my hit."

He looks kind of like a cadaver. His blonde hair is clean but hangs down onto his forehead.

"It's good," he says, and takes another bite of the spaghetti.

"So you played in a band in school?"

"Yeah, all the time. I am good at drums. Always have been. I got hired nearly every weekend. In college I took music classes. I'll get back to it later. My dad and I used to jam. We'll do it again when I'm clean."

"And you'll go back to school. Then get a job."

"I want an M.B.A. I want to be a broker."

"You have two more years' undergraduate then two for an M.B.A. That's not long."

"I want to finish it even faster. My sister says I can live with her when I'm clean."

"Good."

"Where do you work?" he asks.

"Let's always be honest," I say. "I don't trust you yet. I'm not going to tell you anything personal about myself. My friends say I shouldn't talk to you because you'll rob me."

"I've never robbed anyone. I would never rob anyone no matter what. I've never stolen from my parents. I stole from myself. I got cash advances when I got a job. I owed over forty thousand in credit cards."

"Good lord."

"That's cool, though. I understand."

I can tell his feelings are hurt.

"I don't blame you," he says.

He finishes the spaghetti in the large bowl.

"Do you want dessert?" I ask.

"Yes, but let's go somewhere else."

"Sure."

"Let me go to the bathroom first."

"Okay."

I wait while he takes his time. Then he walks back and sits down. The waitress hasn't brought the check. He hasn't fooled me. I can tell by his eyes which are suddenly shining and his cheeks which have color, that he has taken a hit.

"Did you do it?" I ask.

"Yes, in the bathroom. I've done it here before. And next door."

"You just went in and heated some up and shot it in your vein?"

"Sure."

"You're mad. Do you realize that? That's an act of madness. Maybe everyone is mad—they probably are. But your madness is clear. Look at you. Suddenly your eyes are lighted and your face looks energetic."

"I feel tired, just like I looked."

"Where did you shoot it?"

"Here." He points to a place in his arm. "That's a heat rash," he says.

The lumps are not a heat rash. "No it's not," I say. "It's where you got some of it under your skin."

"It goes away. Look here." He shows several lumps along his arms. "The veins get really tough."

"You just went in there and shot up? Why didn't you tell me?"

"Why?"

"I could have watched you," I said, surprising myself. Would I have watched him? Surely not.

"You don't even curse," I say. "You have good manners. You dress well. You know about cultural things. You're getting educated. Yet you do this one thing that controls every little bit of you and fouls the rest. It must be thrilling."

"It is."

"And it ruins everything."

"Yes."

"Well, you have to get off of it."

"I want to. I have to. Then I have to stay off. I've been through detox seven times already."

"Once you get through it you'll be stronger than never having experienced it."

"I know that."

"You ready?"

"Sure."

We head outside. We walk slowly along the pavement. "Show me the syringe," I say.

He takes me over to one side and pulls out something wrapped in brown paper. He unwraps it carefully. "I only use a needle five or six times," he says. "I wipe it off every time."

"Hmm," I say.

"Let me show you the spoon I made." He pulls out another brown paper package and unwraps a spoon fashioned out of the top of a can. Then he wraps it back up.

"You have a blanket where you sleep?" I ask.

"Yes. I even have a pillow. I lay it out real neat. I hate the cold."

"So you go to detox today?"

"I hope so."

"Call me," I say.

"When?"

"Tomorrow about six."

"I will," he says. "Thanks for dinner."

§

The motel clerk says that no William Clark is registered. Hmm, I think, relieved not to meet him. As I walk out of the lobby, headed toward my car to leave, Clark waves at me, standing outside of one of the back rooms. Clark is a professional channeler. I made the appointment for eleven. It is eleven twenty. I have been hunting him for over twenty minutes.

I wave and follow him down the walk and into the dimly lighted motel room. As I walk in, I see the lighted bathroom on our left. "This is my wife Elaine," he says. Elaine is in her sixties, overweight, and making up in front of the small mirror in the bathroom. She smiles, then closes the door.

"If you'll sit here," he says. He has scooted a table to the center of the room and placed two chairs around it. He sits on one side.

I feel sure that I have made a ridiculous mistake.

He closes his eyes in meditation. I watch him brush his grey hair off his forehead then I close my eyes, too. "It takes a few minutes for me to make contact," he says. "I'm not sure who is out there. You have to be careful not to contact an evil spirit."

Not believing a word he says, I nod.

He reaches over, holds my hand, and begins chanting. The words are not unfamiliar, but I recognize nothing. The sounds become nonsensical. He shakes, like he is cold, then slowly opens his eyes. A guttural voice comes out.

Oh my god, I think. The theatricals are as flimsy as the motel room.

"I am making contact," he says. "I am in contact." He opens his eyes. "I am in contact with Herin Zopolater, a soldier in the world army in 2284. He is telling me he has something important for you. Are you ready?"

"Okay," I say.

Clark's entire body shakes. His face reddens, his

eyes widen. Suddenly he closes his eyes. When he speaks, his voice deepens. "There are problems in this year 2284 that were caused by earthlings. Earthlings have committed crimes against existence. They have polluted the environment, stolen from each other, and nurtured poison in their bodies until it is craved and needed.

"I am creating an army of earthlings in 2014 who will become the saviors of the world." He words rush out in staccato sequence. "Earthlings have the most important challenge ever facing them. The challenge is to counter the senseless rape of our natural resources."

He breaks into a language that I have never heard.

"De grono buttich zola ba ba la la dre yu tu." Then he trembles. "You are not to be expected to believe what you hear from me at this time. At some moment in the future when neither you nor I know, you and a group of three hundred loyal followers will be saved while my weapons destroy earth. You will be transported to my ship and taken to another galaxy. It is not important whether or not you believe but you should support the earthly Clark. It is within his power to save you and your family."

I am tempted to get up and walk out, but hesitate. The man is mouthing the words so fast that he could believe he is in a trance and is connected to another being. I avoid looking at him. I hope he doesn't believe this junk. And why am I being polite out of habit?

"The multitude of the world—of worlds, including planets, moons, and spheres that you could not know about are in a period of development we call xintar. This period will bring peace and goodness to the world. The goodness we call pactur. The peace we call pactin. They sound alike because they are alike. The oneness of all will be reflected in this period. Life forms will be freed from violence. There will be no weapons, no strife among the heartless. My apprentice Clark knows about this development. He has been struggling to prepare the chosen for it. He is our appointed leader.

I hear a noise in the bathroom—a commode flushing.

His ego launches into a new subject—the importance of purifying our environment so that we do not poison our children. His eyes remain closed. "All of this is spoken specifically for you James. For your salvation and that of your prodigy. Otherwise all will be lost because of you. Immediately you must change the water you drink, the food you eat, and the products you have in your home. My disciple Clark can advise you on all this. He has accumulated things that will be most useful for you. Do not hesitate to rely on him.

"The god leader of the future has no body but is our model in all we do. We do not have transportation or a genuine means of moving our bodies because the body itself is an organ of the world and the world moves up. Our minds become worn on the outside and the body you see and will see is a mind product. There is no physical other than the loss of memory of our celestial heritage. We must learn to live in a mode that gives our attention not to ourselves but to the things that make up what and who we are: the convergence of all life into each of our perspectives."

Out of the corner of my eye I spot products that he must be trying to sell. Under no circumstances, not even to get out of the place, will I spend another penny.

The clock on the table shows that he continues for twenty-five more minutes and seems to have no thought of stopping. What could his wife be doing? I know that my not leaving encourages him to go on. I imagine what others have said to him. But some—a few—must have been swayed. He is not after the small amount of money I have given him. He wants a relationship whereby he is my guru and I give and give and give to him.

I can not bear another second. His mouth opens and closes, his voice almost supernatural. His vocal strength is remarkable.

When he finishes he has talked non-stop for one and a half hours. My head is pounding. He opens his eyes. He smiles. His voice changes. He has finished channeling.

"He's something, isn't he?" he says.

"Hmm," I say.

"I can sign you up for our newsletter. There are plans where we can buy a property in northern California and prepare for the end."

"I'm sorry," I say. "I don't think so."

He looks surprised. As if I have wasted his time. "At least let me show you some of our products," he says.

I stand up. "Thanks anyway," I say, hurrying toward the door. As I reach it, his wife opens the bathroom door. "Oh, I thought you'd left," she says.

"Bye," I say and step outside. The sunlight is a relief. To be free from that room, from this man. What luck. Imagine if we had to experience everyone's absurdity. Just imagine.

§

At sixty-seven Guido has the lean build of a high school senior. His beard and mustache are neatly trimmed. He dresses well. His waist size of his pants is 29.

"I ran about six miles this morning," he says.

"Where?" I ask.

We are sitting outside of Eurth, a sandwich place in Venice, and the sky is sunny. Every table is filled.

"Over by the Marina."

"How fast?"

"Not very fast. I probably averaged seven minute miles. Keeping in shape when you're older is all about simplicity. Keep it simple. You don't need fancy clothes to exercise. Just do the exercise—run, walk, swim—whatever you are doing, and stretch afterward. You don't need to spend money on a trainer, either, unless you are young and want to look like a professional weightlifter.

"Don't eat too much. Watch what you eat, but first of all, don't overeat. It makes you fat and carrying all that weight around, makes you sick.

"If you want something sweet, try soy ice cream. It's only 2% fat. If you want something different, buy soy ice cream and have half a cup. Once you get used to it, ice cream won't taste so good. It'll be too rich.

"But don't overeat. Spread butter on toast if you like, but make sure it doesn't have salt. Buy bread with the lowest salt. They put salt in everything we eat. When you go to buy some produce, check out what's in it. You don't want to eat something if you don't know what it is. Just keep things simple—eating and exercising. You'll live much longer. You'll feel good."

Later I tell him about Chad whom I'm going to meet. Chad has not gone to the detox as he promised.

"You must not give him money," he says. His expression is a little censuring. "Really, don't do it. You're hurting him when you do. If he doesn't get straight soon, he'll end up in a life of crime."

§

I sit in an aisle seat on row 8 in flight to Los Angeles. A tall middle aged man across from me holds an odd looking electric guitar. He strums the strings with his fingers, playing a song. Then I notice that he wears headphones that look like a doctor's stethoscope. He's relaxing, listening to himself play. No one else can hear him. No sound comes from the guitar. I turn back to my book on Louis XIV; soon I lose myself in the pages. When I look across the aisle again, the man is still playing. It is as if he is giving a silent concert. He glances at me. I look him in the eyes. Then he smiles and nods, pleased to have an audience.

§

The baby the woman holds is swaddled in a thick fleece suit. Little round ears stick up from the fuzzy hood which isn't pulled up over his head.

She holds the child so that its face almost touches hers. Every so often she leans closer, her lips brushing his forehead. The fleece suit is baby blue.

Her long black hair is combed behind her ears. The hair shines and the knot she has fashioned in the back is carefully tied.

Her entire attention focuses on the child. There is no question how much she loves him.

The bus ride is slow and smooth, passing by shoppers who line the sidewalks. She does not glance out of the window. Everything she wants is in her arms.

The boy raises his head, his cheeks revealed to be chubby. He opens his eyes which are quite dark and large. He looks at me for a long while. I feel that I should speak, but I fashion my lips into a slight smile and stare back. He outlasts me. Finally, I look away.

I watch the mother while the child eyes me.

How lovely this woman is, her love an aura around her. She glances at me happily.

The child keeps staring. Who on earth is he? I wonder. When I am dead and this bus is junk, he'll be riding or driving along this road without memory of the rest of us other than his mother. He is not only our future; he is the future. Part of me wants to apologize for looking at him. What is going on inside his head? I am staring my future in the face.

No wonder she holds him so tenderly.

§

I spot a novel by a friend, R. V. Cassill, on a bookshelf across the coffee shop in Venice where I am writing. Verlin Cassill died last spring. I can not remember if I reviewed this novel or not, but I believe it is a weaker one by a brilliant and once well known writer. No one in the coffee shop has the slightest interest in these old books—they contribute to the atmosphere. Their being out of date is on purpose. Each book has had its day. The coffee is what is new.

Six men and one woman around me are busy with their computers. The girl, a brunette, starts to speak to the man in an oversized sports jacket and sweater. He leans back in his chair, looks at me upside down, and laughs. Then they get up and turn toward the door. "Would you watch our computers for fifteen minutes?" the guy asks.

"Yes," I say. "You look different upside down."

I settle back into looking at Verlin's book. Once I told him, "You've been the number one person in our field (of teaching fiction in college) for twenty years."

"Twenty-five," he said.

An undeniable bit of him stands on the shelf, irresistible if you were his friend.

I get out of my chair, walk over, and take the book from the shelf. I read about Verlin: "R.V. Cassill has been a dynamic presence on the American literary scene for more than two decades. As a novelist, short story writer, critic, teacher and essayist, he has set the mark of his imagination on the writing of our times."

I think of how unpredictable it was that so many of his books would go out of print so quickly.

I think how trusting these two young people are who have left me with their laptops.

They return a few minutes later. "Thanks," the guy says. "What are you reading?"

"A book by an old teacher and friend, R. V. Cassill," I say.

"I've never heard of him."

Of course not, I think. How fleeting recognition is. "He published twenty-two novels," I say. I replace the book exactly where it was on the high shelf. It's Verlin's place in this Venice coffee shop. He's still famous in my head.

The man settles down to his computer, uninterested in

the book. I look up at Cassill, glad he is there.

§

The young woman sitting beside me at the counter of California Pizza has a beauty that needs no make up or perfecting. No matter what she wears or what she is doing, she is beautiful. It is her skin color, her eyes, the shape of her face, her lips, her hair, her hands, her shoulders, her waist—it is who she is. You can see it in a glance.

It's seven p.m. on Friday and I feel somewhat lonely eating alone, so I suppose that she probably does, too.

"What kind of soup is that?" I ask, and our conversation begins. Soon I know that she is from Colorado; she works in sales. She graduated from the University of Colorado.

"What gym do you go to?" I ask, a few minutes later.

"I do yoga all the time. And I'm always on the stationary bike at home."

She has the posture of a dancer. "I've just started my own company because I got tired of working all the time and asking for maybe two weeks off a year. I don't want work to control my life," she says.

"No," I say.

"So I'm starting my own company. On a small scale. When my best friend from home was getting married I asked for three days off to fly to Denver. It was a big deal at work."

"Yes."

"My friends all told me—you have great ideas. Go into business for yourself. You'll never get money otherwise."

"What kind of business?" I ask.

"Specialty clothes for children. I want my clothes to be happy—to have a purpose."

"It sounds like a good idea," I say. I'm thinking too, that since I am older and don't want to be seen as a masher, I should talk about my family. "My son is twenty-six," I say. "He's getting a Ph.D. at Vanderbilt."

"He must be smart," she says.

"Yes. And in love. Are you in love?"

"I haven't been for years. But I've been thinking that maybe I'm ready for a relationship again. Someone to call when I get home and say "I'm home" and ask "How was your day?""

"What are your boyfriends like?"

"I met this guy I liked not long ago and we started dating. After a few dates, I asked him if he was dating anyone else. 'Yes,' he said. I thought that was fine, but I liked him and wasn't dating anyone else. Several months later I asked him again. 'Are you dating other women?' He said yes, that he was. So I told him I didn't want to see him anymore. He was surprised and upset, but if nothing had happened for him by then, it wouldn't."

"You'd be wasting your time."

"Wasting my time, right?"

"It's probably harder for you to meet someone in Los Angeles than in a small place."

"It is. At home there are two or three choices of things for me to do. Here there are many. It's more complex. But I get tired of it."

"How about at Yoga?"

"There aren't many men. And they are married."

"The gym? No?"

"Definitely not the gym."

"You should take a class," I say. "Lots of people met in my classes."

"I've thought of that. But I have to decide what to study. I don't want to just take a class."

"You're right."

"I'm not worried about meeting someone. But L.A. can be lonely."

"Yes, it is. It must be especially for you younger ones. So many of you are young. What kind of guys do you like?"

"I want all the usual things. Something just has to happen. I don't have any requirements."

"You should meet someone about thirty-five; not one in his twenties."

"I agree."

"It's wonderful you're starting your own company."

"I've just paid for my first inventory. It'd better work."

"It doesn't do you any good that you're beautiful," I say. "Men feel like they're getting something just taking you out and showing you off. You must never take that for granted."

"I don't even want it. But I know what you mean."

"You must have had to deal with it."

"Of course. But I care about what I'm doing. I don't want anything to control my life—not a job or a boyfriend or money."

"Yes."

"I'm out here on my own for the first time," I say. "I go back and forth to Alabama. I'm independent. I love finding out what I have to think for myself. You've had that."

"Yes, I have."

"It's very important."

"Yes, I forget that."

"It's hard to live in a place where real estate is so high. If you were in Dallas you could buy a condo easily. It would make a difference."

"It would."

"But you know when I talk to people or meet them, it's the street people—those closest to zero—who will tell you they love you in five minutes. Because their lives are taken down to bare essentials. So many people in this city are involved in their pursuing money and fame that they can't— the money and fame won't let them—talk or know people outside that context."

"I wonder what that would be like," she says.

"Excuse me," a voice says. The waitress who serves customers at the counter motions to a line of people waiting.

"Yes," I say. I take the check the waitress hands me and give her a twenty. Then I turn back to the woman on my right. "You really are beautiful," I say.

"Thank you," she says. "I'm late, too. I'm meeting a girlfriend at the movie."

§

The man has a strong German accent. "I am from Berlin," he says. I know no one in Los Angeles, but I go back to Germany, learn English perfect and return. I am German carpenter. What we do. Do you know 'what we do'?"

"Yes," I say.

"I build table or staircase or floor. In Germany I go to school and take master test. You know?"

104

I nod.

"If I say I be somewhere at seven, I there." He stands up from the exercise machine he is using. He is very tall and slim. Serious.

"You see, I start with first job. I do German way—good. Then they tell. They have more work for me. Soon I start company." He has a buzz haircut. "In Germany it is not so. Many people have no work. It is very expensive. There is not work. Of thirty million people, five million no work."

"Goodness," I say. "Yes, in America you can start a company and make money."

"In America there is rich," he holds his hand high, "and poor," he lowers his palm. "In Germany most people middle."

"Yes, the middle class is getting wiped out," I say. "But the American dream is not a myth. Almost anyone who wants to work hard enough can make money."

"I go to bureau for driving today," he says. "License in California is fifteen dollars. In Germany to get license, you take class, you do this, you do that. It cost two thousand for license."

"Good lord."

"In everything—it is law everywhere."

"Bureaucratic…"

"Yes."

"I go back. I study English. To have company I must speak. Not this. Not like now. I talk like American."

"You must learn English," I say.

"First this week I find out about business. I buy car later—five to six thousand. That is good. So I carry tools. In Berlin I drive motorcycle. You know?"

"Yes."

"Big motorcycle. It cost fourteen thousand dollars."

"Goodness."

"I get information so I come back I know. I live in Santa Monica."

"It's expensive here," I say.

"Oh? OK. I live Hollywood. Some place cheaper."

"You can do that."

"Later I live Santa Monica. I marry, have a child. My wife I say I cook. I carry trash. You do, too. We share. I wash clothes. I find American girl."

"They're liberated," I say.

"Yes. Liberated?"

"Free. Independent."

"Not like German girl." He frowns deeply. She not look here or here—only ahead. American girl look at you. She smile."

"Have you met many people here?"

"Only you," he says. "I good carpenter. My father and mother were physics. My grandfather was physics."

"Physics. The science?"

"I say no more. I go other way."

"What does your father do?" I asked.

"He killed," he says. "In Germany cars go 200 kilometers. My mother she was killed…" he smashes his hands together. "My father he die, too."

"Did you have a sister or brother?"

"My sister is two years older."

"How old were you?"

"Eighteen. I eighteen. Very hard."

"How did you find out?"

"I don't understand."

"Who told you about the accident?"

"I was in gymnasium. Not sports. We call school. A policeman came to the school."

"He told you?"

"Yes. I cried. I cried and cried. For a long time."

"How long did it take to feel better?"

He hesitates. "Two years. After two years I OK."

"So you want to start a company?"

"Yes in America you can. My sister—after the deaths, we got close. We stay close always. She worried…you say worried?"

"Yes."

"She worried I come here. She crying. I cried. I call her last night. I come back and learn English," I say. She is very happy. She says 'America is dangerous.' But there are not many police in Santa Monica."

"No. It is a safe place. It is rich."

"Rich. Yes. So they hire me. I've always want to live in America. When I was a boy, I say I'm going to America."

"Yes," I say. "I never thought about where I wanted to live. I didn't like Arlington, Texas. Moving didn't occur to me."

"I start a company in America!" he says.

I know better than to open my mouth and tell this guy what I think the problems of America are. The entire world knows them. We've become a complex, polyglot nation that has lost much of its direction. But this German is kind of a wake-up call—we still live the American dream, don't we?

§

The Japanese sushi cook in Glendale stands at the counter in the tiny restaurant, his face impassive. His black and white checked hat is set straight on his head and his black apron is clean. He watches me eat what he has prepared.

"It's good," I tell him.

"Yes?" he says. "It is good?"

"Yes."

"I am only 5'2"," he says. "I weigh 92 pounds. I eat vegetable sushi like you. I do not get fat."

"92?" I ask. I realize he must be standing on a platform.

"Yes, but I walk a lot. I have no car. I should live in New York City. Every day I walk, walk, walk."

"How old are you?"

"What?"

"How old?"

"Oh no," he says, looking at the waiter standing nearby. He does not want him to hear. Then he picks up a paper and writes 49.

"You don't look it," I say.

"Americans look older because they get fat," he says. "Japanese men do not get fat. They look younger."

"Yes, we do get fat."

"I no go to school. I not educated."

"Can you read?"

"I can not read. I can not write. It is hard."

"Yes. How long have you worked here?"

"Three days. Who knows? You come back, I not be here. But it is OK. Someone else will be here for you."

"Oh you'll be here," I say.

"I work at Hilton before. Very busy at dinner."

"Yes," I say. "Did you like it?"

"No. Very hard work. I fired no English."

I nod. He stands quietly, not acting busy. He takes a deep breath, like a sigh. Then he smiles at me.

How do you tell someone to get educated? I wonder.

§

Riding the crowded bus to Hollywood from downtown, I see a seat in the back open up as the bus stops. I walk over to find that a young black man, just brushing past me, has left his driver's license on the cushion. The license must have fallen out of his back pocket.

I pick it up and hurry down the crowded aisle to return it to him, but the bus doors close as he exits. As we are still stopped, I go to the driver. "That guy outside left his driver's license on the seat," I say, holding it up. I want him to open the doors for me.

The young black driver does not turn my way, but he clearly hears. I'm standing holding the license in clear view. He does not open the doors and the guy has hurried off, unaware of what he has lost.

"Here," I say, "put it in Lost and Found for him, then."

Without speaking he takes the license and as I turn to walk back to my seat I see that he tosses the license out of the window and into the traffic. Then he revs the bus and takes off.

Are we that unhappy? I wonder, sitting down and looking out. I see a man who just got off the bus. He is having trouble with his cell phone. He stands still, then curses aloud, his lips making it easy to see his words.

Maybe we are.

§

I'm on a street off of Broadway downtown, sitting at an outdoor café, having a piece of coffee cake and a bottled water. I notice a shoe shine stand and decide to have my shoes shined. I finish eating and as I walk to the stand, a car honks loudly. I jump, look around, and see no car. Then I hear another honk, closer.

Again there is no car.

The noise must be carrying from a long way away.

Suddenly a siren blares and quickly after, a series of beeps (like unfastened seat belt warnings) occur. Then I see a Mexican walking past. A second later, he makes the sound of squeaking brakes. He is making all these sounds! Perfect imitations.

Amazing, I think. People used to imitate birds.

§

The small pup tent is set up in Palisades Park, across from some of the most expensive condominiums in Los Angeles. I see a young man standing in front of the tent, which is made of white canvas. I can't tell that the man is Japanese until I walk up to him, to warn him of the possibility of being cited by the police. They routinely watch for people trying to spend the night in the park.

"Hey," I say.

"How are you?" he asks.

"Are you traveling?" I see a bike locked to the other side of the tent.

"Yes." He nods eagerly. "I ride bike."

"People aren't supposed to sleep in the park," I say.

"In the park?" he asks, acting unsure what the words mean.

"No sleeping."

"Sleeping?"

"You..." I point to him, then lean my head over like it's on a pillow

"Yes, I sleep in tent."

"Are you Japanese? I've been to Kyoto."

"Ahhh Kyoto."

"Yes, and Nara, very beautiful."

"Yes, beautiful."

"Are you traveling?"

He nods. "Yes."

"Travelling?"

"Yes. I travel. First I in China. I ride bike to Mongolia. Then fly here. I ride bike to Mexico."

"Mongolia? China? You rode your bike in China?"

"Yes, from Beijing to Shanghai. Then to Mongolia."

"Then where?"

"I fly to United States. I go Mexico. One month. Then South America."

"How long in South America?"

"Two months. Then back to United States. Then I ride to Canada."

"How old are you?"

"Twenty-three."

"Do you know anyone here?"

"No. No one."

"Do you have enough money?"

"What?"

"Money. Are you OK?"

"I OK. Money OK."

"How long have you been traveling?"

"How long? What?"

"How long? Time. Months."

"Long time. Yes. I travel long time."

"And you are OK?"

"I OK."

"You are twenty-three?"

"Yes."

"Well, good luck to you," I say.

"Good luck to you," he says.

I walk along the wall overlooking the ocean. I glance back, at his preparing his bed. Isn't that imagination, I think. Yes, it is. What if I had done something like that?
Imagine going to Paris and setting up a tent along the Seine.

§

While I am interested in people and their experiences, I don't feel sorry for them. Rather, I hope to see part of what they're seeing at the moment I meet them, and they can see part of what I am seeing. Each person's challenges are like their shoes—they're theirs. They've walked in them and there's an ownership that you don't share. Their problems are their problems. I am walking in my shoes. They wouldn't want me to wear theirs.

§

How many people do we live with in our heads? The idea is mind boggling. Little children we knew when we were children, schoolmates, relatives, and all the people around us as we grew up, plus those we dated and knew and fell in love with and married, and our children's friends, and our friends and...

§

It is 2 p.m., sunny, and I'm enjoying jogging for thirty minutes along the numbered streets north of Wilshire Boulevard in Santa Monica. The asphalt is easier on the feet than the sidewalk. I halfway glance at the apartment buildings which are alike in their redundancy. Few of the buildings are well-kept, but most of the yards are maintained. I come to a corner, notice a car approaching on my right, and hurry into the intersection, assuming it has a stop sign. Pedestrians seem to always have the right of way in Santa Monica. I feel that I do.

I'm half way across when I turn toward the car. To my surprise it has not slowed down. My eye catches the absence of a stop sign—this is one of the intersections where only cars coming from two directions have to stop. I am in the wrong; the car is not supposed to stop. Nor is it going to.

I hurry, aware that the driver suddenly sees that I am in the street. I think that I can make it across.

The woman goes to slam on the brakes, but suddenly the car rushes at me—accelerating wildly. She has accidentally hit the gas pedal. There is no way that I can avoid being hit.

Damn!

For one instant I *know* that I will feel the impact and then be crushed under the heavy front end. It is happening.

To my horror, I feel the touch of the metal against my hip, my arm, at my waist, and that instant I am lunging, as high as I can, and sail over the passenger's fender. Through the windshield, I see horror in the face of the woman driving. She has long brown hair. A man sits in the car beside her.

I sail over the fender and to my utter surprise, I land on my feet. I feel the hard roadway. I begin to run. I have cleared the fender and am unhurt. If I had waited one instant to jump, I would lie in pieces under the car. The relief is immeasurable.

A few seconds later, I look back. The car is stopped in a dangerous place blocking the intersection. The woman has her arms up, raised into the air, and is screaming. The man beside her yells at her.

Go on, run, I think. End the situation. What would going back do? It would make them worry I'd fake some problem and sue them.

I continue jogging along the street and feel such joy. Most of it is about being alive, a state I had taken for granted a few minutes before the accident.

It feels good to be alive.

The pleasure I feel is the realization that I have saved myself. I was able to react instantly and to sail over that fender.

It is thrilling to have believed in danger and clearly avoided it. Like being in a war.

What a pleasure it is to be alive, I think, as I continue to jog.

§

"I'm not Chicano," he says. "I am from Argentina."

"I thought that was Chicano."

"No, Chicano is Mexican."

"How long have you lived in Los Angeles?"

"Seventeen years. I am a political refugee. In Argentina I was arrested for being a terrorist. I was no terrorist."

"How long did they keep you?"

"Six weeks. They tortured me every day. Electric shock. Beating. Yelling."

"Goodness," I say.

"I was crazy when they let me free. I leave the country, go to Israel."

"You are Jewish?"

"Yes. There are many Jews in Argentina."

"They beat you?"

"Every day. All of us. I heard rifle shots of those they killed. People I meet then, other prisoners, were shot."

"They used electric shock?"

"Yes. Every day. On my testicles. My face. My chest. My mouth. All over me. They said they were going to kill me. I could think of nothing. I was crazy. I was so afraid."

"They let you go?"

"Of course. They realized that I was not a terrorist. After Israel I came to Los Angeles. I found a job; I learned English. In Argentina I was a lawyer. I got a job here working in a kitchen. It was very difficult."

"You like it here."

"Oh, yes. I stay here forever."

"What do you do now?"

"I sell furniture. Every day I thank God for bringing me to the States. I will never go back to my country."

"Is your family here?"

"In Argentina. My mother and father died. My sister lives there. I will go next year for the first time. I do not want to go, but I will, for the relatives."

§

"'It's a boy," I say to the pregnant woman on the elliptical machine next to mine. Her face is covered with sweat.

"Everyone says that," she says, "because of my belly." She sips from the bottled water and replaces it in the holder.

"You have another child?"

"A three year old daughter."

"Good," I say. "You will have a son now." I hesitate, deciding whether or not to tell her an experience I had with my son. "When my son was born," I say, "I wanted to be the first person to see him alive."

"That's a good idea," she says.

"I got around the bed so I could see. Just as the head started coming through, something weird happened. A man's life flashed through me. Like I was living it. I tasted every bite of food he had eaten, knew every article of clothing he had worn, and heard every word he ever said. I experienced every class he sat in, every joke he heard, every feeling he had whether falling in love or feeling angry or whatever. All of flushed through me—it felt as if time were like it is in this life, but it only took a second or two. I understood that the man was dying and becoming my son. He lived in New England."

"Oh," she says.

"I told that to a class I taught once and a woman came up afterward. She waited until every other student had left. She told me that the same thing happened to her when her son was born. Only her husband told her never to tell anyone because it was crazy. She was very relieved to hear my experience… Anyway, every moment of this man's life experience passed through me."

I glance at the woman again. I am continuing to exercise. She has stopped and is standing on the pedals. I don't see that she has any reaction whatsoever. But what could I expect her to say?   "Watch out for it when your son is born," I say.

"I will," she says. She steps off the machine, takes her water bottle and tightens the top.

"What's it like to have a baby?" I ask.

"Not too bad. Only the first few months when you feel sick. Then you become aware that something is growing inside you. By the last month—you're really ready."

"Are you ready?"

"Oh yes, I am."

"Do you dread the labor?"

"No, I'll be glad for it.."

"Good," I say, and wave bye as she walks away. I feel silly, aware there's no way she could understand my experience. Why do I tell it?

§

The men's locker room at the gym is carpeted and has

bright orange lockers. It was recently remodeled. New mirrors and counter tops replaced the old ones. I'm sorting through my gym bag, looking for headphones.

A friend of mine with a mod haircut says, "So you're from Texas. I thought you were from Alabama."

"I grew up in Texas," I say. "I taught at the University of Texas at Dallas."

"Yep. A Texan. I grew up in Riverside. It had fifty thousand then and now has four hundred thousand."

"Arlington, Texas had thirty thousand and now has over three hundred and fifty thousand."

"I read the Dallas Cowboys are moving there," this older man at a locker close to mine, calls out.

"Yes."

"Everybody knows Arlington," he says.

I have seen this man before and clearly he's older than I. I notice he's very fit. "How old are you?" I ask.

He grins before he answers. "Eighty-two." He's proud.

"You don't look eighty-two," I say. I walk up to him. "You have great muscles." I had never noticed. I had just thought of him as an old man—something generic.

He says nothing. Not even, "I used to be in great shape."

"Look at those biceps," I say. "They're bigger than mine." I flex my left bicep and show him. "Flex yours."

He does.

I put my hand over the top of it. The bicep is meaty under the skin, not rock hard but firm. Impressive. The skin around it is loose. "That's bigger than mine," I say. "You have muscles!" I suddenly reach down and press my hand against his chest over his shirt. This is surely very personal. He doesn't

118

object. "Your chest is hard, too. Flex it."

He flexes it.

"My god." I feel of his shoulder and shake it. Strong. "You are in remarkable shape. Maybe I should get busy."

"Thanks," he says.

"Yes, you are," the other man says.

Then I turn and go out the door and into the workout area. Somehow touching him was wonderful.

§

"You look artistic," the grey haired man says as he passes me in the lobby of the doctor's building. I am early for a doctor's appointment and wait downstairs, trying to write.

"Yes?"

"I'm an artist," he says, "I'm seventy-five."

"An artist?" I ask.

"Yes. When I was young I met this man who inspired me. He changed my life."

"I met someone like that," I say. "Who inspired you?"

"An artist named Van Kamp."

"I've heard of him."

"He did motorcycles and cars. Steve McQueen and he were friends. When I met him I worked at a lousy job at a warehouse. He told me, "Get out of this job. Do something for yourself. And I did."

"He was a painter?"

"Yes."

"You've been an artist ever since?"

"Yes. He also told me, don't worry over something. Get it done. Finish it. Go on."

"I was inspired by one person, too," I say. "Do you remember the writer Christopher Isherwood?"

"Yes."

"He liked my first novel. I came out here, met him, and he impressed me so that on my flight back to Dallas I decided to give up my good job and move to Los Angeles. I wanted to be close to Chris. It was the best decision I ever made. Did it change my life!" I hesitated, thinking what to add. How could I express how singular Chris was? His character is always in my head. It still has its effect on me. He was the most generous, caring person I've known. He believed in everyone's integrity. Chris could open his mouth—even at dinner parties—and the truth came out like sunshine. This intelligence was shaped within a wit that never struck out against anyone, yet made all who heard it shake with laughter. Part of being with Chris was uproarious laughter. He understood so much.

"I can't imagine not knowing him. How lucky I was," I say. Instantly I think, is fate luck?

"Me, too," he says, a big smile planted on his face.

I look into his eyes, aware that we are sharing similar feelings at this moment. It makes me happy. Now we either exchange who we are and possibly get together at some point in the future or we can let knowing each other pass by.

I think of my doctor's appointment. Suddenly, the moment has shifted. "I'm so glad to have met you," I say, smiling.

"Me, too," he says. "See you later."

"Yes," I say.

He walks across the lobby and presses the button for the elevator. I suppose he has a doctor's appointment, too. I settle back into my work, a notebook on my lap, a pen in my hand. But I can not think. I take a deep breath. My head is filled with Chris and with a yearning to be in his company again. That's why I wasn't friendlier.

§

The young man across from me has straight chestnut brown hair falling to his shoulders. His thin cheeks have an olive complexion. His blue eyes draw my gaze and keep it. The eyes seem filled with compassion, with an energy that invites anyone to look deep within them.

I stand several feet away from where he sits at an outdoor table, a cup of coffee in front of him. I catch his gaze as I walk up to him. "You look like Jesus," I say.

"I hear that all the time," he says, "but no one knows what Jesus looked like. He wasn't white."

"You look like the picture of Jesus on the wall in my grandmother's house." It surprises me that he doesn't want to look like Jesus.

"Probably," he says, smiling.

I'd like to stare at him for a long while, but that would be more intrusive than I've already been.

"You really do look like him," I say.

"Yeah," he says. "I thought of going as Jesus on Halloween, but I didn't have the nerve."

"My goodness," I say, my long childhood church experience shocked. I can't help but grin at the idea. I nod and walk away. As I do, I wonder what it would be like to look like our pictures of Jesus. He could make a fortune just setting up a stand and blessing others. Would I want to look like him?

Why does this man have that face?

§

The man working out beside me at the gym seems in good shape and is lifting roughly the same weight that I am.

"How old are you?" I ask.

"Sixty-two."

"I'm sixty-five," I say. "You're getting old."

"You know scientists don't know why we age," he says. "We're not supposed to."

"Oh?"

"When we die we've used less than one one-thousandth of our brain. Clearly we were made to live longer."

"But all the other organs of the body wear out."

"Scientists don't know why. Eventually they'll find out how to stop it and people will live a thousand years."

"Do you believe that?"

"Yes," he says. "I do."

"I'd prefer to have multiple lives," I say. "I don't want to keep living the same life forever."

"Think of what you'd learn if you kept using the same brain," he says.

When you get down to it, I think, it's what we don't learn and can't learn that is most important.

"Are you from England?" I ask.

"Outside of Manchester."

"Have you heard of Christopher Isherwood? He was a very close friend of mine. He was from Disley, close to Manchester."

"Yes, I've heard of him."

"He was friends with Auden," I say. I glance at him. "The poet. The British poet." I see he has no reaction.

"Wasn't Isherwood a runner?" he asks.

"He was a wonderful writer," I say.

"Oh," he says, "I thought he was a runner. Anyway, I've heard the name."

I realize he hasn't heard of Auden, either. And I am sure that I haven't heard of who he has heard of…

§

Who are we? you ask. Are we these other people we meet on the street or are they us? Are we interlopers among them? The strangers we meet are some of the most precious gifts we receive: we are allowed to pet the animals. Then we let them go back home without us.

§

The movie theater is dark; the feature is about to start. Everyone in the half full auditorium is settled back and ready. A young man in his twenties hurries down the aisle and chooses a seat on the left. Rows of seats on the right ahead of him are empty.

Immediately after he sits, he mumbles something indistinguishable, then picks up a bag of pop corn that has been left in the seat. He hurls it toward several empty seats in front of him. He throws it like he would a grenade. He catches everyone's attention. Then he takes a cup someone has left in the holder and throws it as far down front as he can.

His manner is violent. In throwing these things he is accosting all of us. He knows it, too.

The young man behind him with a shaved head leans back and grins. Not because he thinks the act is funny. He is grinning at how absurd the man is acting. He glances at me.

I grin, too, sharing the protest. We are laughing about how silly his anger is.

§

Driving back from Hollywood along Fairfax, then on the 10, there seems to be many more cars than people. The only reason I know that there aren't is that somebody has to be driving them. This evening though, technology has raised its skirts and is exposing its privates. There are, at different places, two stalled cars on 10. Traffic is immobile. The predominance of the automobile and its ultimate negative effects are blatant.

Our protesting that no one knew that having too many cars would so adversely affect our society is a weak argument. Technology has won out, just as it is winning in the fields of telecommunications and computer science. Our dependence on technology gives technology dominance over our lives.

Think of how many millions of hours people have worked to pay for these cars and how many million people worked to build them. Imagine the state of our economy without so many automobiles. Or the parts of our lifetimes spent inside automobiles.

The honking and bad tempers the drivers show are other things to think about. They are of course the results of our having created something larger than we are. We become powerless.

The cars barely make a pretense of being beautiful.

It makes you wonder—when we had horse and buggies did the horses love their owners?

§

The young Chicano wears a white shirt and black tie. He stands close by, looking out over the balustrade at the ocean.

"Why are you dressed up?" I ask.

"I'm working," he says. "I have an hour and I came here to see the ocean."

"What do you do?"

"I work for a mortuary."

I'm immediately interested. "What's that like?" I ask.

It's not like what you'd think. I've learned a lot about life working there."

"Have you been in the embalming room?"

"No." He turns and looks directly at me.

"I'd like to do that," I say.

"You have to have permission to go there. I've been thinking about asking. But I'll need some higher up to agree, or maybe I could sneak in. It's a big mortuary. We have several parks."

"Oh." I nod encouragingly. "Have you worked there long?"

"No."

"What's it really like?"

"It's a business. I work in the office. It's like any other job."

"Do you have children?"

"Five," he says.

"Goodness."

"I'm picking up a death certificate from a doctor's office in an hour. Nothing can be done until the doctor signs that the person is dead."

"Where do you live?" I ask.

"In a house. I bought it ten years ago."

"How much is it worth?"

"Half a million. I only owe three hundred thousand."

"How much are the payments?"

"Fifteen hundred a month." He doesn't hesitate answering.

"That's wonderful," I say. "And you can sell it eventually and move to somewhere like Texas."

"My friends have done that. I like it here."

"Where are you from?"

"Mexico. But I've lived here a long time."

"Do you know how they embalm a body?" I ask.

"No. I'd really like to see it. I've been thinking of it."

"Just imagine," I say. And I notice his smile. He doesn't seem to care that I'm interrogating him, although he certainly notices it. But I myself can't think of anything better to ask him. I smile at him and he smiles back and I walk on, wondering how a funeral home became just another business.

§

"I'm ready for a relationship," he says. "I was married for eleven years and have lived alone for fifteen."

"You're tired of being alone?"

His face is sincere. "Yes, I am. I'm ready to have someone else in my life."

126

"Well, who do you want?" I ask. "What kind of woman?"

"Not a fat one. I don't like fat women. My brothers' wives are fat. I can't deal with that. This woman I broke up with during the summer, she called me last night. I broke up with her because she had gained too much weight. 'How's your weight?' I asked her. 'I've gained seventeen pounds,' she says.

"I had to make up every excuse as to why I was not going to be home," he tells me.

"I'm kind of attracted to heavy women," I say.

"Oh yeah?"

"When I was nine and ten I stayed with my grandmother during the summers. She was very fat. At church I used to lay my head on her lap. It was the most comfortable pillow in the world; I got so used to her fat. It was warm and soft."

"I don't want a fat woman," he says.

"My grandmother used to say that skinny women are mean."

"She's probably right. But no fat women for me. I have to defend myself. I'm a little guy."

"You aren't. How tall are you?"

"Five eleven. How tall are you?"

"I'm little; you aren't. I'm five seven."

"I'm little, too."

"No, you aren't. And you should give fat women a chance."

I leave him a few minutes later. Isn't it interesting, I think, how some people hate fat. Is it like hating loud music or bad housekeeping? Why do people hate fat? Fat can be charming and welcoming. And just try cooking as well as my grandmother.

§

I'm sitting by a man who looks half dead at a senior citizen center. His mouth is open; he eyes seem to be closed. He gives the impression of a reptile. His white hair is askew. Blue veins stand out on his hands and run in knots along his legs. He wears shorts, sandals, and a dress shirt.

I can't help but feel sorry that his faculties have left him. He is one of these old men who can sit impassively all day. He sits in front of a set up chess board.

"Want to play a game?" I ask, unsure if he is asleep. I think that paying him some attention is a good thing.

His eyelids open. "Sure," he says, lowly.

"You go first," I say.

"You have white," he says. "White always goes first."

"OK." I move a pawn, then he does. I move another pawn. He moves a bishop. Two more moves later, I realize that he knows exactly what he is doing and I have no idea.

I move a pawn then move it back.

"If you had done that," he says, "I could move here. It's called an impasse. It's French."

"Oh." I am busy defending myself. "What did you do before you retired?" I ask.

"I'm semi-retired," he says. "I'm a dispatcher." He moves his queen, scaring me.

I sit up in the chair, trying to figure out what he is doing. I move my castle.

He moves a bishop.

I move a bishop.

He moves a pawn.

"What do you dispatch?" I ask.

"Taxi's."

"Is that hard?"

"No."

"What are taxi drivers like?"

"People," he says.

He makes a move. I look at the board. Then I see him glancing up at me. Of course he knew I would be no good at chess. He has trapped my queen.

He takes it on the next move.

"I think I just lost the game," I say.

"Probably," he says, with no emotion. He isn't surprised.

I continue to play. I take anything I can of his, but always lose more. "How old are you?" I ask.

"Old enough," he says. "Checkmate."

He is right.

"I'm going to play pool," he says. He gets up and walks off, very slowly.

I think of the utter inertia he showed when he waked up. Was he hibernating? I wonder. Of course I could not have won another game anyway.

§

I try not to show that I am angry. My dental appointment is at nine, yet when I arrive to pick up my car at the hotel garage where I rent a space, it is blocked by another car. Why have the parkers put my car where it can be blocked?

I pay the monthly fees.

"It belongs to an employee," the Brazilian parker says, "but I don't know who. I'll find out. They are supposed to leave their keys, but they haven't."

"I have to be at the dentist in ten minutes," I say.

"Why not take my car?" he asks.

"Oh no," I say. "I don't drive other people's cars."

He nods. "Okay. I'll find out whose car is blocking you."

"Thank you."

He hurries off and I stare at the second hand of my watch. He's certainly being generous, but I don't want the responsibility of driving his car. I want my little car.

He takes longer than I expect to return from the hotel to the garage. It is two minutes until nine. "I'm sorry," he says. "I still don't know whose car it is. I'll have to call the manager."

"OK," I say, in an indifferent tone of voice.

"Are you sure you won't take mine?" he asks.

"All right." I smile, but I am clearly irritated. Why is my car blocked? He didn't do it; it was parked in the wrong place the night before and earlier someone else blocked me. It's not his fault. He is very polite.

"I'll get it," he says.

I'm impatient. He finally pulls up in a four door white Volkswagen. He is especially polite as he opens the door for me.

I get in, the music playing lowly, the black leather seats clean. He closes the door. The keys are in the ignition. I look at my watch..

I pull into the street. The seat is wider and softer

than those in my S2000. The music is soft and pleasing. I like it very much.

I drive slower and with more care than if it were my car. When I stop at the first light, I don't glance at my watch. The music has caught my attention. It seems to surround me in the car, creating an atmosphere quite different from mine. It is like a rural landscape or a gentle rain.

When my battery died two years before, the radio stopped working. I could not find the code and decided I preferred the silence, at least as long as I was aware of it.

But this voice on the CD is so pleasing. Relaxing. Being in his car tells me something about him. What taste this young man has. His English is not good and we have hardly spoken. He is tall, dark, good looking. He seemed reassuring. His car shows something remarkable.

I suddenly like him. I sit back in the luxurious seat and feel pampered by the music. In fact, I'm experiencing a moment of joy. Who cares if I am a little late? Had I rather be hurried and anxious or relaxed and impressed?

I take a deep breath. I appreciate this man's generosity, too. I want him to buy several CD's for me. He knows what I like better than I do. Some girl is going to be very lucky to marry him, I think. I let the woman's voice on the CD lull me, and when I see an empty parking space in front of the dentist's office, I pull into it and shut off the ignition. I sit several minutes. I hate getting out of the car. I have been some place intimate, despite the traffic, my hurry, and every emotion I was feeling before. What a joy it is to be in the context of this person. Then I think, but we're in the contexts of other people all the time—just think of how often they delight us.

§

The man in the bright red Christmas sweater is short and happy-faced. He looks as if he is always cheerful.

"For years I lived just below where the Getty Museum is now," he says. "I don't much like the look of the new building. There was a hermit who lived in a cave where the museum is. He was a kind man, but he never spoke to me. He would wave or nod—and most of the time he stayed in the cave. They had to get rid of him, of course, to build the museum. I have no idea where he went.

"Mrs. Getty was a wonderful person. One afternoon she was driving past my place and she saw me in the garden. She had the chauffeur stop the car. She got out and walked over to me. 'So you like gardening?' she asked. 'Very much,' I said. 'I've always loved it.' 'I'm glad to know that; you have a beautiful garden.' I thanked her and she got back into the car and traveled on. A few days later a truck pulled up and a group of men got out. They began to tear down the fence behind my small garden. Then they took new boards and built an entirely new fence, greatly increasing my garden. I rented the house from her. Anyway, the garden was much enlarged. She came by later that afternoon and said, 'Now you have a much bigger garden.' I thanked her. That is what Mrs. Getty was like."

The man beams a kind of happiness. I couldn't help but think that Mrs. Getty was responding to that as well.

END

On James White's *Birdsong*:
(ISBN# 0-916092-30-5)

"What a delight even if a *difficult* delight ! it must have been to write it!" -Gwendolyn Brooks (Pulitzer Prize winner)

"I loved it all the way through." -Christopher Isherwood

"A poignant reenactment of a rite of passage, fragile and joyous as the title." -*Library Journal*

"The novel is a masterpiece of simple beauty...you cannot put *Birdsong* down." -*El Paso Times*